Last of the Baronites

Novella #3 in THE DEER KING Series

I0621366

Ben Spencer

ISBN-13: 9781732038028 (Paperback)

KNOCK-KNEE BOOKS

To be notified when a new book in *The Deer King* series is released, visit benspencerwrites.com and follow the blog.

OTHER BOOKS IN THE DEER KING SERIES

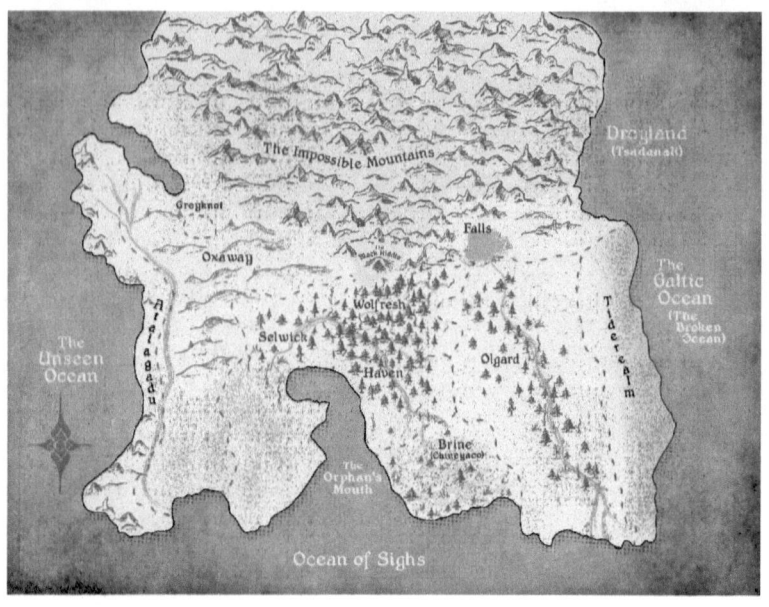

1

January, 200 A.D. (After Drey)

Owen Walsh awoke with a start. Someone was sitting on his bed.

"Father?"

"Yes, Owen. It's me."

Outside, it was dark. Owen's internal clock told him that it was a dead-of-night darkness, not a pre-dawn gloom.

"Is something wrong?" he asked his father. It was a stupid question. Of course something was wrong. Daybreak promised the dawning of a new era in Olgard, an era in which William Walsh would no longer be the president. An era in which the Free Harrish, and not the Baronites, would have complete control over the government.

"I'm leaving," William Walsh replied by way of an answer.

"Now? In the middle of the night?"

"Yes. Now."

Owen nodded in the dark. He was nineteen years old, a man grown, but he had never felt more like a boy at that moment. His father, the outgoing president, was returning home to Smoketon, while he was to remain in Centichester, the capital, to be thrown to the wolves.

"Don't leave until the day is done. If you leave now, they'll lambast you in the press. General Burgod stayed for your inauguration. They'll say that you should have stayed for Mr. Randolph's."

"And what of it?" William Walsh replied, discharging his signature snort; the blast of air from his nostrils sounded like a slap to the face. "If they do write about me, it will be nothing more than dancing on a dead man's corpse. Better that than having to suffer the indignity of pretending to accept the ascension of that calumnious pack of liars."

A bitter silence hung in the air like acrid smoke. Owen wondered if a whiff of it would hang around his father for the rest of his life.

"You did what was right. You kept us out of war."

William Walsh's hand flew from his son's shoulder, a wave of dismissal in the night. *His Demonstrativeness*, a Free Harrish rag had once nicknamed him. It was among the kinder of the monikers the Free Harrish had conjured for William Walsh over the years.

"Yes. Of course," William said dismissively, as if keeping Olgard out of war with Tiderealm had been a simple matter. "Just as you'll do right when I'm gone, both for Senator Stevens and for the country. You're a Walsh. Being a Walsh means standing on principle when others bow with the tide. It means keeping your honor and dignity even when circumstances compel you to do otherwise. Do you hear me, Son?"

"Yes, Father. I do."

An uneasy silence descended. William Walsh sensed it.

"I'm about to leave, Son. If there's something you want to ask me, ask it now."

"It's nothing, Father. I understand what it means to be a Walsh. I understand what I'm supposed to do."

But how do I keep my honor if I'm challenged to a duel? Owen had wanted to ask. But he didn't. Somehow, in all their talks the esteemed William Walsh had never found it pertinent to advise his son on the matter of dueling. Owen knew that his father thought dueling stupid and barbaric, but when William Walsh was coming of age, duels weren't as common as they had become of late: these days, the slightest provocation was grounds for a mortal engagement, and worse, rash young men with a deadly shot and an eye for advancement often thought challenging a famous name to a duel as the quickest way to climb the political ladder.

And there were few names more famous than Walsh.

His father patted him on the shoulder. Owen looked to his father for some sort of reassurance, but William Walsh was already turning away, his eyes hungering for the door. Even in the dark, Owen could see the pained look on his father's face. Owen understood why it was there. This should have been a joyous day for William Walsh. His long and distinguished career in politics was finally over, only, instead of leaving with the knowledge that he had brought his political visons to fruition, he was turning the government over to those who would shortly undo much of his life's work. The history that William Walsh had long tried to usher into being was turning against him. And, in the short term at least, his reputation would suffer for it.

"Be strong, my son," William Walsh said. Then he stood up and left.

Owen lay in the dark, not moving. He had dreaded this day for weeks. His father's presidency was over. The Baronites were no longer in power. And the Free Harrish were eager to feast on the spoils of their victory.

The future was here. And Owen Walsh would have to face it alone.

The eleven Baronite senators who had survived the election were already in the Pit when Owen arrived at the Beacon Building. They were a glum-looking lot, these titans of the age, reduced by the change in the political tides from proud, staunch protectors of the Baronite Philosophy to dispirited has-beens. Glancing about, Owen scarce recognized half of his father's former allies. Senator Whitestone, known for his impeccable style, was dressed as shabbily as a pauper; Senator Thumb, whose acumen was most often compared to sharp objects, stared dumbly into space; and Senator Moxley, who normally carried himself with aplomb, was surreptitiously picking his nose.

Owen searched the room for his father's man, who was also his new employer. Senator Jude Stevens. When at last Owen spotted the senator, he was sitting, of all places, in the vice president's seat at the head of the chamber, his granite jaw jutting so far out that it appeared to be commandeering the room.

Seeing the old battle horse stiffened Owen's spine. *At least one Baronite isn't cowed*, Owen thought, but that thought was quickly followed by a different, more worrisome consideration: *He isn't planning to stay in the vice president's chair when the Free Harrish arrive, is he?*

Owen rushed down the aisle, the dull percussive thump of marble underfoot. Senator Stevens gave him a cursory glance as he approached, then went back to the task of fixing his jaw. The senator's dogged browns were glued on the heavy oak doors that led into the chamber; no doubt he meant to stare down the two men who would shortly be taking their oaths of office in the same spot the senator was sitting on that very moment.

The incoming vice president: Rufus Arry.

And the incoming president: James Randolph.

"Is your father gone, boy?" the senator growled as Owen approached. His eyes never left the front.

"Yes, sir," Owen replied, coating his voice with a thin layer of ice. He was young, but he would hear no ill words spoken of his father. Not from a fellow Baronite, at least. Not today.

"Can't say that I blame him. Still, I suppose that leaves it to me to give the Slavocracy the greeting they deserve. Free Harrish, my old, wrinkled ass. The only freedom these tyrants wish to bestow is the freedom to put a heavy yoke on whomever they please. Titan save our republic, but were he in his infinite wisdom to make me king for a day, I'd rid the country of this scourge…"

The doors at the back burst open, letting in a joyous sound that swelled as the men responsible for the noise trailed it into the chamber. Owen turned with the rest of the Baronite faction to watch their adversaries enter. Leading the way was Tyus Redgrave, the twenty-four-year-old son of the late Secretary of State Daniel Redgrave. A weasel to his father's fox, Tyus had declared himself a Free

Harrish man shortly after his father's death, completing the decade-in-the-making transition of the Redgrave name from the Baronite to the Free Harrish camp. Today he was reaping the rewards: Tyus was youngest of the newly elected Free Harrish senators.

Tyus, who with his dirty-blond hair and bulky build looked like an overfed lion, spotted Owen straight away. They had known each other for years: long ago, Owen had considered Tyus Redgrave something of a boyhood idol, but that was before the events of the previous decade. Tyus gave Owen a smile, but his was of the curled-lip variety, the sort of leering, predatory grin that meant nastiness was in the offing. As the remainder of the Free Harrish contingent poured into the chamber, Tyus made a beeline for Owen, breaking his gaze only long enough to steal the occasional glance at Senator Stevens.

"What is your man doing up there, Walsh?" Tyus said as he approached, jabbing his finger at Senator Stevens like it was a sword. He wore a mask of feigned anger, but he wasn't fooling Owen. Underneath, he was all joy.

"The Honorable Tyus Redgrave," Owen deadpanned in reply. He simultaneously bowed out his chest at Tyus while letting his eyes go heavy, trying to act defiant and unconcerned all at once. It wasn't easy. Tyus was six-three, a mere inch shorter than his legendarily tall father had been, while Owen was only five-six, the same height as his sire. *His Diminutiveness,* Owen thought, remembering another of his father's nicknames. It wasn't one of the more popular nicknames, but it had had some sticking power nonetheless.

"Tell your man to move, Walsh. The new president is coming."

"You misunderstand the nature of my position, Tyus. He is not my man. I am his. If you have a problem with where Senator Stevens is sitting, I suggest you take it up with him yourself."

Tyus cringed at that. He might have been bully enough to try out his tough talk on Owen, but it was another thing to trade barbs with the combative and silver-tongued Jude Stevens.

"Fine," Tyus replied. The smirk in his smile blossomed. "Come to think of it, perhaps this is for the best. I can think of no better way to usher in this glorious new era than watching old Jude Stevens embarrass himself. Let's view it together, you and I. Two young men, one with his future ahead of him, the other—what are you Owen, nineteen years old?—caretaking for a faded relic, his best days already behind him. President Randolph should be entering soon. In fact, there he is now."

And so he was. Rufus Arry was holding court in front of James Randolph, glad-handing all comers with his customary mustachioed vitality, but now the Free Harrish were getting wind of Randolph's arrival. A smattering of handclaps quickly turned into an avalanche of applause. Vice-President Arry, realizing he was blocking the president from view, stepped out of the way so that the chamber could see James Randolph in full.

There's the man who destroyed my father's life, though Owen. But looking at James Randolph, it was difficult to believe that he was capable of such vicissitudes. With his pale, nearly translucent skin and plaited red hair, the president-elect looked more like an exotic plant than a rough-and-tumble politician. He had always had a refined quality, but there were times when that same aspect blurred into an unsettling ephemeralness, making Randolph appear alien, near unhuman. He looked that way to Owen now.

"Man of the people, my ass," Senator Stevens growled from behind. Tyus wheeled on the old man, seemingly prepared to defend the president-elect, but, realizing that only he and Owen had heard, he decided against it.

Randolph acknowledged his many loyalists in the chamber by raising his hand without quite waving, and dipping his chin without quite nodding. Then, along with Arry, he began making his way down the aisle.

They were halfway to the dais when all at once the room came to realize that Senator Stevens was sitting at the front. The senator rose in response. Owen, a spectator along with the rest, watched as the old warrior took firm hold of his jacket lapels and struck a formidable pose. He wasn't a very handsome man, nor was his frame particularly daunting, but, even now, at the nadir of his political career, when Jude Stevens demanded the attention of his colleagues, he received it.

Rufus Arry stopped walking down the aisle, as did President-Elect Randolph. Arry, who had always had a quick tongue—if not the quickest of minds; there were many in his own party who thought him a policy hack—struck first.

"Why, Senator Stevens," the vice president elect intoned in his Roseville drawl, "we may yet let you switch parties if you make a strong enough case, but I must insist you wait at least six years before taking possession of that particular chair."

There was an outbreak of laughter from the Free Harrish faction in the room. But, when Jude Stevens refused to respond to Arry, it quickly died. Jude Stevens turned his unforgiving gaze on the president-elect, and, like a righteous prophet come down from the mountain, declaimed.

"And so you've won."

An uneasy silence filled the chamber. James Randolph, his countenance relaxed, stared pleasantly at the senator, but said nothing.

Senator Stevens gave a dismissive little snort. Then, with his graying curls frothing on the sides of his scalp like waves in a tempest, he pulled a paper from his jacket pocket and waved it in the air. "I have in my hand a peace treaty signed by King Hugo Whesker of Tiderealm, a treaty negotiated by our outgoing President Walsh, a treaty that you and yours did your damnedest to hang around President Walsh's neck for the purpose of costing him the election. I ask you, sir, before you come forth today to take the oath of office as this nation's president, will you respect the terms of this treaty once you are sworn in?"

Owen looked at the president-elect. For months now Randolph had stood to the side while his lackeys did everything in their power to sabotage the peace negotiations, including but not limited to fomenting fears that, were the treaty signed, Walsh would declare himself a monarch like Whesker, and the two of them would make common cause against their pro-slavery enemies. Only yesterday William Walsh had signed the treaty, his last act in office. And now, in the blink of an eye, Randolph might undo it all.

But to Owen's surprise, with a soft voice, the new president said, "I will."

Owen, struggling to process his own reaction, was distracted by the murmurings as they swam around the chamber like a school of fast-moving fish. Try as he might, he couldn't discern agreement from discontent. His father had told him it was a possibility that Randolph would uphold the treaty—James was a pragmatic man in his heart of hearts, and the treaty was a boon in reality, no matter how the Free Harrish had tried to depict it—but to hear the new president admit before the entire Olgardian government that he meant to abide by the very treaty that his party had railed against for the better part of a year was too infuriating to be entirely a relief.

Up on the dais, Jude Stevens didn't move. He stared impassively at the president-elect, a giant star in the solar system, waiting patiently while the minor bodies in the room were once again sucked into his gravitational pull. Satisfied that he had reclaimed their attentions, he delivered his final, cutting lines.

"Titan bless you, Mr. President, for saving the Olgard union." A hairsbreadth of a pause. "And Titan damn you for your treacherous hypocrisy."

They wanted to kill him. The twenty-one newly elected Free Harrish Senators and their ilk all heaped on the abuse, cursing, shouting, baying, waving their fists in the air, threatening bodily violence, making it known that Jude Stevens would pay, like the pagan god Cairth on Felling Day, he would pay. From beside Owen, Tyus Redgrave unleashed a string of invectives so blood-curdling that Owen felt a shiver go up his spine. On some faraway planet, a thought occurred to Owen. *Perhaps I should go to the man.* He didn't want to come to the senator's aid—it was suicide—but the Walsh sense of duty was a powerful thing. He felt his feet moving forward, toward the dais, compelling him to doom.

But then, all at once, the chamber grew quiet.

Owen turned toward the silence.

James Randolph had his hand in the air.

When the new president spoke, his voice was stronger than before. "Senator Stevens, your lifetime of service to our nation has earned you the right to speak your mind. As yours is a mind that I hope to call upon from time to time, I hope that party politics will not impede our ability to form a relationship conducive for the good government that we both aspire for our country."

If the Free Harrish were disappointed by their leader's temperate words, they didn't let it show. A chorus of "Hear, Hear" quickly broke out, accented by the percussive rumble of walking canes on marble. Where only moments ago there had been a chamber full of bloodthirsty hounds, now there were only indignant gentlemen, waiting for the senator from Smoketon to right his wrong. All eyes went back to Jude Stevens.

The old codger didn't give them the pleasure of a reply. Instead, he silently refolded the treaty, briefly raised it aloft for all to see, and placed it on the rostrum. Then, with cold gray eyes appraising his manifold enemies, he departed the stage.

A couple of boos rang out as Senator Stevens stepped down, but the heart for it was gone. Instead, the celebratory impulse ascended once more. James Randolph and Rufus Arry resumed their historical walk to the quickening cheers of the Free Harrish throng. By the time they had reached the dais, the huzzahs were loud enough to wake the dead.

Owen stood still as the pageant unfurled. All the major players passed him by. Jude Stevens without word or eye contact. Arry, arrogantly. Only Randolph gave Owen a look, a minor-key glance of recognition before resuming his stroll toward history.

As Owen watched the new president and vice president position themselves to take their respective oaths, Tyus leaned into his ear. "To think that they were all friends once. My father. Yours. Mr. Randolph. And General Burgod, of course. The generation who led us through the Sovereignty War. But that story has already been written, hasn't it? And now we watch another begin. The dawn of the Free Harrish, the death of Baronism." Tyus Redgrave paused, and smacked his lips ever so slightly. "Look at them up there. Life's a crowded stage, my dear Owen.

"Not enough room for us all."

2

On the fifth day of Free Harrish rule, as the party went about the business of disbanding the High Federal Court for the purpose of turning judicial power over to the cities and provinces, Owen could take it no more.

"I need to leave," he whispered to Senator Stevens as he leaned over the senator's desk and handed him the horror script that was the following day's agenda. "A break, until…"

Jude, his stone-like gaze fixed on some distant, eternal hellscape, granted Owen's request with a rough flick of the wrist.

Owen's desire to flee the chamber as quickly as possible outweighed any shame he felt at not being able to bear further witness to the dismantling of his father's legacy. For days Owen had watched with dismay as the Free Harrish attacked the past with a butcher's glee, hacking to pieces nearly all of the Baronite Party's major legislative accomplishments. Gone were the Olgardian Acts, the Baronite legislation meant to bind the country together. Funding for the Great Roads Project had been gutted. The bill establishing the Olgard Naval & Military Academy had been repealed. And today, Titan save them, the Free Harrish were disbanding the High Federal Court, meaning that in effect each city and provincial court would be free to interpret the constitution according to its own discretion.

And now Owen had seen tomorrow's agenda.

The Slavocracy was going to have its say.

Hurrying out of the chamber, Owen veered left, toward the great colonnade overlooking the Marinus River.

The colonnade was one of the many flourishes the famed Trufic architect Alexander DuContirs had added when he designed the government building—now known as The Beacon—back in 174, before the Sundering. The Ithiaian columns harkened the past while being firmly entrenched in new world soil; approaching the columns, it was easy enough to believe that one had stepped back in time to the Ithiaian Republic, but, once aside the pillars, the sight of the powerful, rushing Marinus disabused one of the Ithiaian aesthetic: nothing in stony, mountainous Ithiaia was the equal of the new world river, neither in force or vitality.

Owen took up a position near the center of the colonnade. The morning sun cast light on the striated rock that ran from The Beacon's eastern base all the way down to the Marinus. Near the river, a group of women were dipping wooden bowls into the shallows. The women, clad in black and white, took turns pouring bowls of freezing water over the top of each other's heads.

The Titan's Daughters. Owen watched the holy women go about their morning purification rituals with a fascination that wasn't entirely devoid of prurience. His eye was drawn to one of the women in particular, a teenage girl perhaps a few years his junior. She seemed out of place compared to the others: although she willfully submitted to the ritual, the very essence of her being seemed to rebel against it, from the rigidity of her carriage to the stony aspect of her eyes to the way her brown, windswept hair danced in the wind right up to the moment the water streamed over her head. Even after the ritual was finished she stood out: as the women exited the shallows, she fell to the back of the line, seemingly for the purpose of stealing left and right glances at the world around her.

The sight of the girl agitated him. Something about her being a Titan's Daughter: she was too young, too bursting with life to have made such a commitment. *Most likely she's an orphan,* he thought, trying to formulate a justification on the girl's behalf. He felt guilty for feeling the way that he did—he was an adherent of the Bronze Titan, after all, and he knew in his heart of hearts that his frustration at her station wasn't entirely separated from his sexual desires—but being aware of the less-than-pure reasons for his agitation did little to quell it.

He was continuing to track her progress up the western banks of the Marinus when a quartet of men descended on the sandbar from the north. Three of the men were dressed like gentlemen, clad in telltale breeches/waistcoat finery, but the fourth wore a rough piece of white homespun. Furthermore, upon closer inspection, it appeared that the fourth fellow wasn't entirely of Harrish descent: he looked Torquecan, or, to be more precise, Torquecan-ish. *Perhaps he's of mixed descent,* Owen conjectured, though the moment the thought entered his brain, all hell broke loose.

The quartet, which up to that point had been engaged in an ill-defined conversation, abruptly split in half, as one of the men grabbed the Torquecan and pushed him roughly down the river bank. The respective duos, now separated, suddenly produced a pistol apiece. The two gentlemen on the upper end of the river made a smooth, premeditated show of it: one handed the pistol to an expectant other, while downriver, the Torquecan, who had by then stumbled to the ground, found himself on what appeared to be the unanticipated receiving end of a proffered gun.

They mean to murder the man, and make it look like a duel, Owen managed to think before the first shot rang out.

The pistol fired.

The Torquecan, struck by the bullet, writhed in pain on the ground. Some of the *Titan's Daughters* screamed.

Owen watched in horror as the Torquecan's second encouraged him to return fire. The second's patience, however, was as short-lived as it was fake: grabbing the Torquecan by the hand, the second jerked the Torquecan's gun skyward. A harmless shot discharged into the air.

Upstream, the gunman readied his second round. Finished, he took aim at the Torquecan once more. Unhappy with his odds of dealing a lethal blow at the present distance, he took two steps forward.

Murder, Owen thought yet again. He stood stupefied as the man prepared to pull the trigger.

But then, out of the corner of Owen's eye, a blur of black and white.

The girl Owen had been watching earlier crashed into the gunman with all her might.

Owen stopped watching, stopped thinking, and started moving: he cleared the colonnade and began navigating the rock-laden rise, trying to get to the river as quickly as possible without breaking a leg. Down below there were screams and shouts, but no further gunshots.

By the time Owen reached the shore, the scene was different than it had been from on high. The Titan's Daughters, spurred to their sister's defense, had formed a half-moon around the gunman, who had a hold of the girl and was refusing to let her go. The Torquecan lay wounded on the ground, half-conscious and bleeding from a bullet wound in his left thigh.

The Torquecan's second was sprinting away, down the southern banks of the river. Owen thought he recognized the man, but, in the madness of the moment, he couldn't place him.

"Unhand that woman!" Owen shouted as he approached. His head swiveled between the respective parties.

The men, trying to suss out Owen's station, refused to respond; they merely stared back at him with mean eyes. Owen got his first close look at the key players. The gunman was a short but strong piece of work, with the look of a pampered bullfrog. The gunman's second was a lanky scarecrow of a man: although dressed in nice enough clothes, his unkempt hair and coarse beard still managed to convey a sense of overall shabbiness.

The girl—who for the moment had stopped struggling with the gunman—looked like a crescent moon on a clear winter's night.

"Unhand her, damn you!" Owen shouted again. He was torn between coming to the girl's aid and checking on the wounded man. He stopped near the Torquecan and leaned over him, trying to ascertain the extent of the damage. He caught a glimpse of the Torquecan's full face and lolling eyes; for the briefest of moments, he thought the Torquecan looked familiar. But there was no time to figure it out. His eyes went to the wound. The bullet had bored deep. Owen wasn't a doctor, but his initial impression was that an amputation might be in order.

"Careful."

The Torquecan's strangled whisper so confused Owen for a moment that he didn't realize it was the wounded man who had spoken to him.

Owen whipped his head back around.

The tall man was conferring with the short one, whispering rapid-fire into his ear. Bullfrog had a panicked look in his eye, and he was toying with the gun in a way that made it clear he was considering using it.

Owen said the first thing that came to mind, the words pouring out of him in a hot rush. "I am Owen Walsh, son of the second president of the Olgardian Republic, and I swear to the Bronze Titan that if you don't unhand that girl and drop your weapon, I will use every resource at my disposal to see you hanged!"

That did the trick. Bullfrog let go of the girl, who, to Owen's amazement, appeared in no hurry to get away. She simply stood there with a look on her face that bespoke a resolve to see the gunman undone, with no thought to her personal danger. It wasn't until one of the Daughters stepped forward and grabbed her by the arm that she moved from the Bullfrog's side.

Owen sensed others gathering on the periphery. The gunman and his friend did too. After a couple of anxious looks over the shoulders, they decided it was time to go. But before he left, Bullfrog made a declaration.

"Today I defended my honor in accordance with the code of the duel. Let it be known!"

Then, turning on his heels with his second, he fled the scene.

All soon became a hubbub. Those on the edges moved in, while in the center the Titan's Daughters surrounded the girl, urging her away.

Owen turned his attention back to the Torquecan.

The wounded man gathered his lolling eyes long enough to focus on Owen and say, "I am a true free man."

Then he passed out.

Jude Stevens held the tumbler of whiskey in his hand with a loose sort of menace, the way a gladiator might hold a mace. Everyone in the capital knew that the senator considered alcohol the scourge of the earth. That fact, however, had never stopped the senator from partaking of the occasional drink.

"You say he was a free man? A true free man?"

They were standing in the senator's office, located in the Beacon's western wing. It was late evening—outside, the sky was ripening dark.

"That's what he said. On the river bank and at the doctor's."

"Did he give you a name?"

"Charlsey Roges."

"Sounds Breekish. You said he was a Torquecan?"

"Half-Torquecan, I believe."

"Hm." The senator swirled the whiskey in his glass absentmindedly. Owen knew what he was thinking. If the man was half-Torquecan, and, as he claimed, a true free man, chances were he was the issue of a slaver and a contracted woman. "Go on, tell me the rest."

Owen took a deep breath through his nostrils. The rest was the hard part. "Charlsey said that when he arrived at work this morning, one of his coworkers pulled him to the side. Before I say more, you should know where Charlsey works."

"Yes?"

"The Anti-Monarchist Herald."

An absolute stillness settled over the senator. Owen knew better than to think it was calmness—he could see the rage in the old man's eyes. And for good reason. No Centichester rag had done more damage to the Baronite cause in the previous election than the *Herald*.

Owen continued. "Charlsey delivers the papers. It's been his job for five years. Today when he arrived at work, his coworker, a man named Duncan Broggs, pulled him to the side and told Charlsey that he might be fired."

"Broggs. I've heard the name. One of the editors, I believe. A contemptible scoundrel, no doubt, like the rest. What reason did Broggs give?"

"Delivery failures. He claimed there had been complaints. He suggested to Charlsey that they go out and meet with the customers together. Charlsey was dubious. He knew that he had made all the deliveries. But, being half-Torquecan, he understood that he couldn't speak to the customers alone. So he went along with Broggs."

The senator took a sip of his drink. The whiskey's gaudy hue mimicked the color of the wood paneling in the office.

Owen continued. "To Charlsey's surprise, they met up with the first so-called customers on the road. Two men, one of whom Charlsey recognized immediately. Not as a customer, but as the fiancé of Amelia Redgrave."

Senator Stevens frowned. As his expression was usually some variant of a glower, his actual frown was severe to the point of looking inhuman. "The story can't get better from here."

Owen was blunt. "No, sir. It cannot." Amelia Redgrave, they both knew, was Senator Tyus Redgrave's younger sister, a twenty-year-old debutante. Owen had had a crush on her when he was younger, much the same as had any young man who made her acquaintance.

The senator knocked back the rest of his drink with a grim duty. "All right," he growled, pointing the now-empty tumbler at Owen. "Let's hear the connection."

"Charlsey's mother was a contracted worker for the late Daniel Redgrave. Charlsey, as you may have already guessed, was released from his contract shortly before the secretary's passing and made a true free man."

"Titan save us—he's the secretary's bastard. And a half-brother to Tyus and Amelia."

"In all likelihood. Though Charlsey himself wouldn't admit to it. When I asked him where the Roges name came from, he said it was the surname of his father, a contracted Breekish worker who died years ago."

Stevens harrumphed. "Breekish paternity certainly provides a handy answer for the question of one's complexion."

"It does."

The Senator half-slammed the tumbler on his rosewood desk. "Keep going. I'll not jump to conclusions, tempted though I am."

Owen nodded. "The name of the man who shot Charlsey is Lucien Gringer."

"Any relation to Jasper Gringer, the banker?"

"Lucien is Jasper's nephew. Charlsey said that when he ran into Lucien on the street, Lucien kept up Broggs's ruse about the newspaper deliveries. He even pretended that he didn't know who Charlsey was while the three men badgered him toward the river. But in truth Charlsey had had a long discussion with Lucien only two days prior. You see, Charlsey is in love with a young woman who is currently contracted to the Redgrave family. Charlsey wants to marry her. As such, he told Lucien that he'd like to buy out her contract when Lucien marries Amelia Redgrave. He was under the impression that Lucien was amenable to the idea. That is, until this morning."

Stevens's frown hardened on the tableau of his face, great cracks of dry earth on a sunburned plain. "Damned fool. Discussing the matter was the height of stupidity. He should have waited until he had the money and demanded her freedom right then and there. The law states—"

Owen interrupted, "—that a contracted worker may not be denied their freedom if an offer of marriage by a true free person is made along with sufficient recompense for the remainder of the contracted worker's contract, sufficient recompense being determined by the Olgard Contract Exchange." Owen thought it worth the cost of the senator's glacial glare to finish the sentence for him. The senator was a good man, but he was prone to elucidating on the finer points of legalese ad nauseam, as if Owen wasn't William Walsh's son.

The senator, glaring at Owen two or three seconds longer than was necessary to make his point, picked back up the thread. "And now the picture is complete. The duel was meant to be a fait accompli. With Charlsey dead, the living could put words in his mouth. Broggs would use the *Herald* to paint the man as if he were the demon-god Cairth himself, yet another child-snatching true free Torquecan come to rob the honest men of the world of their contractually obligated workers. Tyus Redgrave would rid himself of the half-brother he never wanted. And the Free Harrish would have ammunition for the bills they mean to pass next—rolling back the laws protecting contracted workers to the degree that they'll be slaves again in all but name."

"It's a fine distinction, as it is."

"First rule of politics, my boy. Matters can always get worse."

The senator was insufferable at times, but, as usual, he was right. From the time Owen was a boy he had watched the Baronite Party struggle to pass legislation protecting the newly freed Torquecan slaves, always with fierce resistance from the Free Harrish, and sometimes even from members within their own party. In the coming days, it appeared that even those weak-tea laws would be swept away.

"Has the leg been amputated?" the senator asked.

"Not yet. Doc Bickerstaff fished out the bullet, and now he's keeping an eye out for infection. Charlsey's femur is shattered. He was resting when I left."

The senator narrowed his gaze on Owen. "Tell me you didn't leave him alone. Tell me you kept eyes on him."

Owen shifted uncomfortably. "Doc Bickerstaff is watching him."

The senator pointed a gun-barrel finger at Owen. "That sexagenarian is no more capable of protecting the Torquecan than he is of curing the common cold."

"I'll go back this instant," Owen said. He had already turned for the door.

"No!" the senator shouted. Owen turned to see that beads of sweat had broken out on Jude Steven's forehead. "I'll be damned if I'm the man who sends William Walsh's son to his death. You keep away. Especially now that it's dark. Go fetch Gringold instead."

Owen felt a prickle of relief, a prickle of shame. He had played the hero's role all day, but night brought with it different circumstances, different beasts. A man like Gringold was more suited for the task at hand. Gringold knew how to handle himself under cover of darkness.

"Yes, Senator," he replied.

For the second time, he turned to go.

Gringold was a half-Breekish, half-Harrish heavy, loyal to the Baronite cause for complex reasons that were more personal than political. He reacted to the news that he was needed to guard a wounded Torquecan man whose life was in danger as if he had been expecting it all evening. "Tell the senator that when the sun rises, the Torquecan will number among the living," Gringold said when Owen had finished his spiel. Then he rolled his massive shoulders and set off for Doc Bickerstaff's, taking his eerie formality with him.

The moment Gringold left, the full weight of the day's burdens descended on Owen. Instinctively, Owen tried to channel his father's voice. *Bear up. You're a Walsh*, he told himself. But surprisingly, it didn't do the trick. Quietly, beneath a dark and moonless sky, Owen slumped to the ground and put his head in his hands. He may have even cried. He was on the brink of succumbing entirely to his emotions, when he tried his father's voice again.

This time the old Walsh fortitude won out. He stood up and started walking.

Gringold lived about a mile west by northwest of the Beacon building, along that nebulous Centichester line where the governmental areas merged with the city proper. Gringold's residence was one of the so-called *skinny shacks*, long and narrow wooden homes that were popular among the working class. As Owen walked away from Gringold's, he felt the barometric pressure in his body shift, the dense weight of urbane humanity giving way to the thin, rarified air of the political realm. The vistas were better on the governmental side of town, but that didn't mean the air was easier to breathe.

Owen's current residence was about half a mile upriver from the Beacon, in the guest house of a grand riverside estate that predated the Sovereignty War. Owen had lived there for the past three years, having left his previous home—the presidential palace commonly known as the Gray House—halfway through his father's term. His current residence was, like most houses in the northern side of the city, Baronite-friendly: the estate had once belonged to the man many considered the father of the modern Baronite Party, Brigand Potter. The childless Brigand was long dead, but his identical (and now ancient) twin Mathias was still alive. As had long been the case, Mathias provided free lodging in the guest house to young Baronite strivers making their way in the world.

Currently, Owen was the only resident.

Owen angled northeast, thinking to hurry home and make a night of it. He was both tired and hungry, and he knew odds were high that the morrow would birth new stresses sprung forth from the belly of today's drama.

But on his way, Owen's attention was drawn to one of the few non-governmental buildings in the governmental district, the Temple of the Bronze Titan. The temple's many windows were alive with candlelight. Gilded, fully-lit candelabras resided both in the windows that ran along the temple's slender, stone-white sides, and in the windows in the front, a stacked pyramid of glass meant to represent the Bronze Titan's all-seeing gaze. During the daytime, the windows faded into the recesses of the white stone, but at night they became the fiery eyes to the temple's soul.

The temple sat on a sprawling plateau of grassy land downhill of the Beacon. Owen's intention was to steer north of the temple, but the closer he drew, the more the candles attracted him like a moth to the flame.

Or so he told himself. In reality he was curious about the girl.

He wondered if he would go inside. The temple was open at all hours to those seeking succor, but Owen wasn't a lost soul. He was a president's son; as such, he went to temple on High Auten Mornings and Felling Day, and that was it. To go to the temple at a different time was to risk being seen at the temple at a different time. For the Walshes of the world, this simply wouldn't do.

But the girl! He would stop in and say a prayer. Or…better yet, he would stop in and ask to see the girl directly. He had reason, didn't he? The priest on duty would recognize him—*Yes, that's right, I am William Walsh's son. There was an incident this morning, down by the river. One of the Titan's Daughters was involved. I need to speak to her*—and then…and then what?

He would talk to her. He would ask her why she did what she did.

Doubts crowded in the back of his mind, roosting bats ready to fly from the mouth of a cave, but he was running now, toward the candles, desperately trying to outrace second thoughts. He was at the front of the temple before they could catch up to him, and then he was pulling on the massive dew oak doors, and then he was inside.

And there, unbelievably, was the girl.

She was standing in the middle of the temple, dusting pews. Looking around, Owen saw that she was the only woman in the room. Two supplicants were praying at the front of the temple, and a young priest—who must have drawn the short straw for nighttime duty—was walking the aisles. The priest and the girl looked up at Owen when he walked in, but only the priest held his gaze; the girl went back to her work.

The priest approached. He was a thin man with a bulging, too-large nose and long, spindly arms. He concealed the extraordinary length of his arms by holding his hands together near the center of his chest. Owen thought that the young priest's name was Debin, but he was by no means certain.

"My dear sir, if you've come to pray—" the priest broke off, a look of recognition dawning on his face. "Oh my…Mr. Walsh…my apologies, I…seeing you here is a surprise, is all. But…many pardons…all are welcome at all hours—" the young man was rambling, "—and it's so very good that you've come to pray. Which aspect of the Titan—"

Owen interrupted. "Priest Debin?"

The young priest's eyes lit up in gratitude. "Yes! You remember my name! Quite the memory you have. But that's no surprise, considering who you are."

Owen tried not to grimace at the flattery. "My apologies, but I haven't come to pray. That young woman over there? She—there was an incident this morning— perhaps you've heard—and I wondered—I had hoped—" now he was the one rambling incoherently, "—perhaps I could have a word with her? I was there, you see, and certain questions surrounding the event linger."

He sounded like an idiot. But, looking at Debin's too-eager lapdog face, he thought perhaps he was in good company.

"Oh yes!" the young priest replied. "The incident! It's why Emmaline is cleaning the temple tonight. High Priest Musk was none too happy when he heard. But between you and me, I've never seen a Titan's Daughter so fully embody the Titan's formidable aspect. Everyone has noticed it."

Owen nodded. The fear he already felt at the thought of talking to the girl spiked at the mention of her formidability.

The priest continued. "As for your request—who am I to reject the wishes of a president's son? Go talk to her."

Owen nodded again. His nerves were turning him into a creature of brusque efficiency. "Thank you. I won't be but a moment."

The girl—Emmaline, was it?—looked up at Owen as he approached. She slowly narrowed her eyes at him, until, with a pupil-expanding *pop*, she made the connection. He had hoped that when she recognized him she might offer him a thankful smile for his role in helping her earlier that day. But no. Instead she stared at him with a resolute sort of toughness.

She spoke before he did. "Did the man survive?"

"Yes," Owen managed. He desperately wanted to look at her, but he was finding it difficult to meet her eye for more than a fleeting second. "He's under the care and supervision of a doctor at the present moment. The biggest worry now is infection."

She gave him a curt little nod. He steeled himself and looked at her full-on. She had striated green-brown eyes framed by a crescent-moon face; together they formed a sharp-edged visage that stopped short of looking severe. She was of average height, and, as best as he could tell in her black and white robes, lean in a way that called to mind predatory cats. He thought that she was beautiful, perhaps even more so because he imagined hers was a beauty few others would appreciate.

"You're the president's son," she said. It was a statement, not a question.

"My father is no longer the president," Owen replied. "But I am William Walsh's son."

He waited for her to say more, but that was it. Instead, she continued staring at him with an unrelenting gaze. He finally looked away, wondering where she found the audacity. Owen knew grown men who had difficulty carrying on a conversation with him on account of who his father was, let alone meeting him eye to eye.

He summoned his nerve yet again, and made eye contact once more.

"You were brave this morning," he said. "You saved that man's life."

She responded as if she hadn't heard the compliment. "That man was a Torquecan, right? I imagine that was why they were trying to kill him."

"Based on what I've been able to gather, his race did play a role, yes."

"Hmm. Will anything happen to the men who tried to murder him?"

Owen was taken aback. Even after seeing what she had done this morning, her forwardness still startled him.

"I don't know. I hope so. I've spoken to people…we're trying to get to the bottom of it. But the world is not always just."

She gave him a cold little smile. "Wise words from a president's son."

Was she mocking him? Her smile and tone suggested this was a possibility, but she had threaded the needle of her response so that it was impossible to deduce her true meaning. Whether intentional or not, her words cut him. His wounded pride spurred him to boldness. He suddenly knew exactly why he was here. What he had come to ask her.

"Why did you join the Titan's Daughters? Are you an orphan?"

He felt ashamed the moment the question was asked. What type of man was he, to ask a young woman he didn't know such a personal question? But, to his surprise, she didn't flinch.

"Yes. I *am* an orphan. I lost my mother when I was a young girl. My father died a little less than two years ago. He was the Stoneman in Haven. When he died, I wanted to honor his memory the best way I knew how. So I traveled to Centichester, to begin my journey as one of the Titan's Daughters."

Owen was stunned. "Your father was the Stoneman?" *The last Stoneman? The one killed by the renegade priest?* Owen knew the rough details of the story. Besides the threat of war with Tiderealm and the mess in Brine, nothing had tormented William Walsh his last few months in office like trying to get to the bottom of what had happened in Haven.

"That's right. We lived in Mossbane, on Haven's northern border. Along with my brother." She paused. "He's dead too."

"Oh…my condolences." Owen didn't know what to say, only that he had a million questions, none of which were proper to ask. "I can't begin to imagine what you've been through. I'm glad you've made it here. It speaks highly of your character that you made the decision to become a Titan's Daughter. Pardon me if I'm out of place, but I'm certain your father would be proud."

The expression on her face was inscrutable: the initial effect was a stoic one, but there was a secondary quality as well, a strange impish look that belied the first impression. He didn't know what to make of it. Was she lying? Toying with him? The girl was maddening, maybe even mad, and here he was standing in the Temple of the Bronze Titan in the dead of night being made a fool of…

"It's difficult to know what my father would have thought. But truth be told, I don't intend to remain a Titan's Daughter for much longer."

Oh. Her whispered words explained everything. Owen searched the periphery for prying ears, found Priest Debin attending to one of the supplicants at the front, a gentle hand on the man's shoulder while the praying fellow beat at his chest.

"You're leaving the sisterhood?" Owen asked, whispering back. "But how? I thought that when a woman became a Titan's Daughter, she became one for life?"

She smiled, a Titan's honest full-fledged grin, lovely teeth that flashed and then disappeared like a chimera. But when she responded, she ignored his question entirely. "I read the letter your father wrote to the Massaporan people after the Saving Stone went missing. Usually it's hard to get your hands on the printed word out on the frontier. But President Walsh's letter was everywhere."

The letter. Owen remembered it. A simple piece of diplomacy meant to buy time while William Walsh focused on more pressing issues. He looked at her curiously, wondering why she had made such an abrupt pivot to politics.

The girl continued. "At first I didn't grasp that the letter wasn't actually intended for the Massaporan people, even though it was addressed to them. Your father was writing to the Havenese. My people. The settlers. When he appealed to the hearts of the good Massaporan men and women who cherish the peace won by the Wolfresh-Potter Accord, he was actually trying to assuage the fears of the Havenese."

She was right. Above all else, Owen's father had wanted to avoid a bloodbath. He wrote a letter to the Massaporan people that he knew only the settlers would read, in the hopes that it would temper their anger sufficiently enough that they would stop calling for a full-scale invasion of Wolfresh. Addressing the letter directly to the settlers would have infuriated them. But addressing it to the Massaporans gave the Havenese the necessary remove to reconsider their rush to war.

"Then your father sent the soldiers."

The girl's words threw Owen. Being the Stoneman's daughter, he would have thought she would have approved of the small platoon William Walsh sent to Haven. But her eyes said otherwise.

"If my father hadn't sent the soldiers, the Havenese would have taken it upon themselves to go into Wolfresh," Owen responded. "That would have proved disastrous."

She smiled at him again, an enigmatic grin. Try as he might, he was finding it exceedingly difficult to get a grip on her true nature.

"I left for Centichester the day the soldiers arrived," she continued. "As such, I've only read the newspaper reports of what happened. *A surgical response*, the newspaper said. *Only one village razed*. Your father, it seemed, was right about the good Massaporan people. From the sounds of it, it was the Massaporans themselves who pointed the soldiers in the direction of the *Dachahelu* worshippers."

Owen felt punch drunk. How had they ended up on this topic? And this girl, this Titan's Daughter?—who was she, really? *Emmaline*, he reminded himself. *The priest said her name was Emmaline.*

The girl glanced over Owen's shoulder. Owen followed suit, saw that Priest Debin was headed their way, an ear-to-ear grin on an inquisitive face. The young priest's curiosity was getting the better of him.

Owen turned back around. To his shock, the girl was standing close enough to give him a kiss.

"You said I was brave this morning. You were brave too."

"Thank you," Owen replied.

Another pocket of silence. For the first time, the girl looked uncomfortable. It seemed the giving and receiving of compliments didn't suit her.

The priest was closing in, twenty feet away.

Emmaline's face flashed with...panic? But only for a moment. She had been struggling over a decision, Owen conjectured, but now the decision was made.

She leaned into Owen's ear.

"The new vice president meets with the High Priest weekly. They're discussing what to do about Wolfresh. Whatever it is, it's going to happen soon."

The words spoken, she stepped back, gave him a soft look, and then turned and departed, marching past the bemused priest, who seemed to consider stopping her but ultimately thought better of it. Owen watched with wonder as she kept going, disappearing into the bowels of the temple behind the apse.

Owen was fairly certain that he had fallen in love.

The young priest chuckled as he approached. "If she told you what you wanted to hear, you'd be the first. Formidable, that one. Brutally honest too. A true Titan's Daughter, if you're partial to the old scriptures. Between you and me, she'll be the death of the High Priest. The old man says she's giving him ulcers."

Owen nodded, though he scarce heard a word the priest said. He was too busy replaying the conversation with Emmaline in his mind.

3

The morning was a riot of sunshine and news. By the time Owen made it to Senator Stevens's office, half of Centichester had read the blaring headline on the front page of *The Anti-Monarchist Herald*.

TOAD KING'S SON STOPS HONOR DUEL TO SAVE TORQUECAN RAPIST

ANOTHER TYRANT IN THE MAKING?

The old man was reading a copy at his desk when Owen walked in. He looked up long enough to give Owen a bizarre smirking smile and the paper a good shake. Owen wasn't certain, but he was fairly sure the senator was trying to conjure an expression that conveyed a sense of pride.

"Toad King. Ha!" the senator shouted. "The Slavocracy is in charge of all and still they resort to juvenile barbs. As if your father hadn't peacefully left the presidency. But crows will caw. It is in their nature, after all. And you, young man…a tyrant in the making? Why, the Free Harrish are so unfamiliar with altruism and bravery that when it's thrust in their faces, they have no choice but to brand it something altogether different! Don't you worry, my boy, I've sent word to the ink hounds over at *The Daily Centichester*. Our version of events will hit the streets by midday."

Owen was formulating a response when a shadow devoured his body whole. He turned to find Gringold entering the office behind him. The big man's expressionless mug gave away nothing. On anyone else, it would have been cause for concern.

"He's still alive, then?" the senator asked, a low-pitched growl in his voice.

"The Torquecan lives," Gringold replied. He was a large man, no doubt, but Owen thought he was made larger by the oddity of his behavior; his size and personality accented one another, the two characteristics working in tandem to reinforce Gringold's uniqueness.

"Last night was quiet?"

Gringold took a seat on the Carver chair in the corner, his massive thighs crowding the wooden arms. The senator cringed, but made no comment. Gringold leaned forward, resting his arms on his knees.

"There were prowlers. Prowling. Might have been cats. I banged pots in the street loud enough to disturb Cairth down in the Bottom Black. It did the trick. All quiet after."

The senator harrumphed. "You might have nabbed one of those prowlers for what I'm paying you. Gave us a look at who our antagonists are sending."

Gringold shook his head. "These cat-men were paid to spy, not to kill. I ruffled the owl's feathers, to ensure the hawk never came."

This tortured bit of wisdom was too much for the senator. "Yes, yes, and if you spank a pig on its ass you'll firm up the sausage. See, we're both wise men. I trust the two I sent to relieve you this morning paid proper coin?"

If Gringold was offended by the senator's slight, he didn't show it. He simply nodded yes.

"Good. Be ready again tonight. I'll send word by sundown."

Gringold stood up and took his leave. Upon his departure, the room felt twice as large.

"Charlsey Roges is safe, for now," the senator said once Gringold was gone. "And we have work to do. Today is the day the Slavocracy means to start destroying the republic in earnest, and I won't have you running off again, not even if you sniff out another duel. Now, I doubt the Free Harrish will be so bold as to propose restoring slavery in whole, but without a doubt they're going to attack the contract system—"

"Senator," Owen interrupted.

Jude Stevens flinched at the interruption, then glared at Owen. "Out with it."

"Last night I—" he hesitated for a moment, suddenly nervous about telling Jude Stevens where he'd been, "—stopped at the temple on my way home."

"The temple?" For a brief moment the senator's ever-present irritability was replaced by confusion.

"Yes. The temple. There was a young woman, a...um...Titan's Daughter—"

The look on the senator's face changed from befuddlement to a pained horror. "Merciful Titan, boy, if you mean to tell me that you've fallen in love with a holy woman, I beg you—"

"No! No. That's not it at all. This young woman was a witness to the duel, and I had hoped that she might spread a little more light on what occurred. But when I spoke with her, she shared information that I wasn't expecting. She said that Vice President Arry has been meeting in secret with the High Priest, and that they've been discussing the Wolfresh situation. She said that whatever it is they intend to do, they're going to do it soon."

The senator chewed on this, looking like a man suffering from an ulcer. "Not much to go on. Do you believe her?"

"I don't know very her well, Senator, but...yes. I do believe her. She had no reason to lie."

The senator gave his desk an angry little slap. "That damned priest. Ever since the giant Kern died out in Mossbane, Musk has had his heart set on a proper invasion. He's convinced there's a newborn Deer King on the loose, no doubt. Him and every other holy man on the continent." He stood up all at once, in his customary huff. "As if our work wasn't cut out for us enough this morning. All right, then. Arry didn't have the votes for a full-scale invasion the last I checked, but I'll do a little reconnaissance before session to ensure that's still the case." His spiel finished, he gave Owen one last stink-eye. "Why a Titan's Daughter felt the need to divulge that information with the son of Olgard's second president is beyond me. Hopefully I'll never know. Just remember you're a Walsh, son. Live every day pretending as if your father is staring over your shoulder."

Owen gave the senator a stiff little nod. He wanted to say *There's very little pretending involved*, but he knew the satisfaction it would give him wasn't worth the trouble it would stir up.

Besides, they needed to get going. There was work to be done.

The chamber that morning was fraught with a strange intensity. The Baronite faction, who should have been disheartened after days on end spent racking up legislative losses, looked rested and battle-ready. The shock of being in the minority had at last passed, and, aware that today's votes weren't a foregone conclusion, they were spoiling for a fight. The Free Harrish, conversely, entered the chamber considerably more uptight than before, the weight of the historical measures they were proposing clearly burdening many of them. A handful of the Free Harrish—Tyus Redgrave among them—enacted shows of confidence, strutting about and laughing with their caucus, but, if anything, their ersatz élan only emphasized how different today actually was.

And all of this was before Jude Stevens went to work.

Owen had his own to-do list, but first he watched the senator. The old codger spent the morning giving marching orders to the Baronites, one or two of whom peeled away to find cause for conversation with select Free Harrish. These were special cases only. The other Baronites—the majority—whispered words to their chief adjutants, who then made their way to the rotunda outside the chamber, and there exchanged select bits of intel with their Free Harrish counterparts—hushed, hurried tête-à-têtes that were in no way binding.

Owen kept his eyes on the senator while the others hustled to the back ahead of him. His part of the plan wasn't set to begin until Jude Stevens sat down.

When at last the senator eased into his seat, Owen began his stroll.

As expected, the scraggly, grey-haired Abner Cox—a Sovereignty War vet who had once been a national hero before being disgraced by a sex scandal, and was now the chief adjutant to Senate Majority Leader Briggs Shroud—followed suit from across the aisle. It was tradition for the two adjutants of the Majority and Minority leaders to speak to each other before a session began. Their conversations were usually short and perfunctory: the Free Harrish, generally speaking, had no need of Baronite votes, so there was usually nothing to discuss.

Owen felt confident that today would be no different. Which was to the good, because it wasn't Abner Cox that Owen needed to speak to.

They opened doors on opposite sides of the chamber and emerged in the rotunda, where a robin's-egg blue sky poured through the windows high above. Cox gave a little sneer as Owen approached. The two men could not have been more different. Cox was the oldest adjutant in the chamber, and, comparative to the others, from humble origins. Owen, on the other hand, was the youngest adjutant, but the most pedigreed, and arguably the most polished. Even at nineteen years old Owen had more diplomatic experience than many of his counterparts (courtesy of his two years spent as personal secretary to the ambassador to Tiderealm from the ages of eleven to thirteen), and his political expertise was obvious enough to anyone who spoke to him. Cox, however, didn't care. He thought Owen a nepotistic little shit, and took little pains to hide it.

"Mr. Cox," Owen greeted Abner in a soft voice.

"Master Walsh," Abner replied. Cox loved to mock Owen with the childish honorific. Owen, accustomed to it, paid him no mind.

"No pressing message from your side of the aisle, I assume?" Owen inquired, keeping his tone neutral.

"Actually—" Abner replied, looking uncomfortable as he stared off into space, "—Senator Shroud wants me to pass word that if the old coot Stevens will allow a voice vote on the morning's first two bills, the senator will be inclined to open up the floor this afternoon, should your side take issue with a bill."

Owen sensed a trap. "The agenda this afternoon is wide open. Everything of consequence is on the morning docket."

Abner flashed a pair of high eyebrows at Owen. "So it seems."

The word "Wolfresh" crept to Owen's tongue, but he didn't speak it. At best, the word might buy him a read on Abner's reaction, but Owen didn't think it worth the price of cuing the Free Harrish onto their best guess.

"You are lacking in specifics, sir. The only conclusion I can draw is that Senator Shroud isn't certain of his votes. You should know better than to think Jude Stevens will do your dirty work for you."

Cox fixed him with a cold stare. "We have the votes, boy. Call off the dogs this morning, or face the consequences this afternoon. Tell your man."

Cox stalked away. Owen turned in the opposite direction, and walked toward the bronze statue of General Norman Burgod, first president of the republic, standing guard at the doorway to the outside exit. Despite the present circumstances, Owen couldn't keep from glancing at Burgod's face. As always, the first president's imperious gaze refused to meet his own. Burgod's expression didn't match Owen's boyhood memories of the man. A long time ago, Owen had asked his father if the general was a sad man. After he had recovered from his surprise at the question, William Walsh's answer had been blunt: *"Yes, I believe he is."*

Owen hovered in the statue's shadow, keeping his back to the room. Seconds later, a pair of colleagues sidled up beside him, one friend and one foe. The foe's question was direct. "I need confirmation, Walsh. Braswell here says that if my man kills the contract bill, your man will provide the votes needed to oust Briggs Shroud as majority leader?"

Owen kept his eyes on the general's boots. "Confirmed," he replied.

The pair slipped quickly away.

Owen let his eyes wander north, where the general was still staring off into some distant plain.

One seed, thrown to the wind, he thought. *Let's hope it bears fruit.*

Jude Stevens said not a word when Owen told him all had gone according to plan. He simply grunted and sent Owen on his way.

The first measure the Free Harrish introduced that morning proposed putting an end to the practice of declaring any slave who had escaped from Tiderealm a true free man. Henceforth, all runaway Tiderealm slaves would be held in custody until such time as they might be returned to the Whesker Kingdom, or, if that were unfeasible, until they signed a labor contract in Olgard.

Jude Stevens didn't object when Briggs Shroud motioned to bypass debate and proceed with a voice vote.

The Ayes took the vote, one side of the chamber in a chorus of agreement, one in a chorus of dissent. The Slavocracy victorious. Owen grimaced as he watched Tyus Redgrave deliver hearty backslaps to his bench mates.

The second measure was the contract bill. Vice-President Rufus Arry, sitting like a showy vulture up on the dais, slicked his moustache with forefinger and thumb before reading the bill to the chamber. For once, his syrupy Roseville drawl didn't work on the room like a soporific.

"Henceforth, any Harrish man offering a labor contract to a non-Harrish worker has the right to add a lifetime stipulation to the contract, thereby ending the seven-year maximum contract condition set forth in Bill thirty-one. Furthermore, all current seven-year contracts may be amended to include a lifetime stipulation. Any laborer who refuses to sign the amended contracts serves thenceforth at the discretion of the guarantor, who may honor the original contract or terminate it according to his desires. Any and all uncontracted non-Harrish workers must apply for true free status within ten days of their contracts ending, and, if the status is so granted, pay the one hundred fifty gold mark fee at that time. All undocumented non-Harrish workers without true free status must leave the state of Olgard immediately. Any non-Harrish worker found in Olgard after the twenty-day grace period upon the expiration of a contract may be placed under arrest until they either produce sufficient payment to register as a true free person, or until they agree to contract terms with a Harrish guarantor."

Owen was taken aback. The bill went further than he had thought it would. It restored slavery in all but name.

Senate Majority Leader Shroud, who, with his small stature, looked like a handsome mushroom made sentient, eyed Jude Stevens from across the chamber, and made another motion to bypass debate and proceed to a voice vote.

"Not this time," Stevens growled before the motion could be seconded.

"This bill is going to pass," Shroud said in response. "We'll give you your debate, Jude, if you put it to a vote, but that's the only vote you'll win. So why don't you and yours save your energy for other matters."

Jude said nothing. Shroud sighed, cast his eyes to the heavens. "The motion is tabled," he declared. "All right then, Senator. Let's begin."

The orator of the ages struggled to an upright position, readying a speech against slavery that would no doubt echo down the corridor of Olgardian history. But, for once, Owen wasn't watching Senator Stevens. Instead, he used the moment to steal a glance at the hinge on which their ploy to stop the contract bill hung. The man whose adjutant they had tried to bribe this morning. The man currently sitting beside young Tyus Redgrave, a man who—by Jude Stevens's count—commanded five of the twenty-one Free Harrish Senators (six including himself). A man who wouldn't tip his hand during the debate but who might turn enough votes their way to carry the day. Senator Sterling Holmes. Back-channel negotiations had been ongoing for weeks, and Owen's confirmation this morning was the signal that it was time for Holmes to play his hand. If all went according to plan, Sterling Holmes would be the new majority leader by the end of the day, courtesy of the Baronite party coming to his side to make common cause with the five senators in Holmes's pocket.

A new party would be formed. It wouldn't be the Baronite party of old, but it wouldn't be the Free Harrish party either.

But first Sterling Holmes needed to show Jude Stevens that he had the guts to abandon his party and stop the contract bill.

And this was the moment of truth.

It was tempting, when Jude Stevens was speaking, for Owen to regress to a boyhood state, to believe that men were reasonable and moral creatures who might yet be convinced by the heartfelt and self-evident truths pouring from the senator's mouth; that, when at last the senator was finished speaking, the chamber would stand in unison and declare as one that neither slavery nor the criminal labor contracts that kept the Torquecan people in bondage would ever be permitted in the nation of Olgard again.

But as the senator's sterling words faded, as the self-evident truths he had lain bare for all to see dissipated into the murky and unknowable past, as the old warrior settled back into his chair to cede the floor to those who were already chomping at the bit to do their damnedest to undermine the senator's moral claims, Owen knew that at the end it would come down to matters of self-interest, such as whether Sterling Holmes thought sabotaging the contract bill was worth the price to advance his political ambitions. Three Free Harrish senators were already expected to vote against the contract bill. They were all Holmes's men, of course, and all hailed from provinces or cities in the northern half of the country. But, for the bill to fail, the Baronites needed all six of Holmes's men to play turncoat, including Holmes himself.

When debate resumed, the fire-eaters took up the cause. Senators from far down south—namely the city of Roseville and the province of New Glowerglass—rose and with a collective militant mind castigated Senator Stevens with all the might the Bronze Titan's formidable aspect could impart to their tongues, railing against his claims of moral certitude with the self-righteous zeal that can only be summoned by those whose wickedness has been exposed. After an hour of this, a handful of Baronites rallied to Jude Stevens's defense, but their speeches were paltry imitations of the original, and, knowing as much, they didn't talk for long.

At last, an uneasy quiet descended. Majority Leader Shroud gave the room a quick once-over and pounced.

"I make a motion that we proceed to a formal vote. In addition I'm asking my colleagues on this side of the chamber to defer to Senator Stevens for the second."

Senator Stevens, hunkered down in his chair like a burrowed badger, allowed a considerable amount of time to pass before replying.

"I second the motion."

The ayes were unanimous. Owen, standing in the back with the other adjutants, was suddenly overcome by the vote's importance. This was it, he realized. The last stand of the Baronites. They would either win here, or they would cease to be a factor as a national party.

Seemingly apropos of nothing, Senator Shroud stood. Something about his posture unsettled Owen.

"I'm using my prerogative as majority leader to ask that the vote count be tallied by geographic region rather than alphabetically, starting with the Northern provinces and cities and progressing to the south."

Why? Owen thought. It made Owen wonder if Shroud was onto them. But even if he was, what did it matter? In a moment the perfidy of Holmes's men would be revealed, and then what recourse would he have?

Rufus Arry peered down from his perch at the front of the chamber. Owen thought he saw a sly fox's grin emerge from Arry's mustache burrow, before the vice president went about the business of rearranging his call list.

Owen checked Senator Stevens. The old war horse's expression was indecipherable.

The room went as still as a winter field the moment the snow stopped falling.

Arry cleared his throat. "Senator Moxley, from the province of Devinsgard."

Moxley, with customary style and grace, rose from his chair, took hold of his jacket lapels, and said, "Nay."

And so it went. The Devinsgard senators all voted against the bill, both the three Baronites and the one Free Harrish. The Four Smoketon Senators voted nay as well, Baronites all.

No surprises yet.

White Ruins, the province surrounding Centichester, came next. Both the Baronites voted against the bill. Then came the Free Harrish. The senators were both Holmes's men, but only the first, Paul Thomas Tice, had made it known that he was against the bill before the vote. Tice's vote recorded, the vice president called on Edward Mountbain, the first man who needed to switch his vote if the plan were to succeed. Mountbain, a vainglorious popinjay who loved nothing more than to hear the sound of his own voice, for once, looked terrified to speak.

"N...N...Nay," he said at last, voice and legs quivering as he took his seat.

There was a minor reaction, a few raised voices and one audible gasp, but it was nothing like Owen had anticipated. A handful of senators on the Free Harrish side looked confused, but most did not. If anything, Briggs Shroud looked grimly pleased.

Shroud looks that way because we've unsettled him, Owen assured himself. *He doesn't know what's happening.*

Next came the senators from Centichester. Arry called on the ever-dapper Aaron Whitestone, a Baronite, first. A sure no vote. Rather than watch Whitestone, Owen fixed his attention on George Conway, the next Free Harrish man who needed to jump ship for their plan to succeed. He was only half listening when Whitestone spoke.

"Aye," Whitestone said, a guilty tremble in his voice.

The stunned silence that fell over the chamber was unlike any Owen had ever heard before. It was the sound of disbelief, the sound of betrayal, the sound of the end of the Baronite Party. While they had been plotting ways to steal votes from the Free Harrish, the Free Harrish had stolen one from them.

And it only took one vote to undo their plans.

Jude Stevens broke the quiet by thundering his fist on his desk. Then there was shouting, slander, even a wail of woe. In the midst of the hubbub, Isaiah Braswell, one of Owen's fellow adjutants, came over and grabbed him by the arm, a frantic expression on his face.

"Are we finished?" Isaiah asked, a pleading note therein.

"Yes," Owen replied. "That's it. Slavery is restored in Olgard. And the Baronite Party is dead."

Holmes and his men reversed course. They summoned their collective thespian skills and voted "aye" to a man, leaving Edward Mountbain to twist in the wind. Vice President Arry declared the final vote count nineteen to thirteen, and proclaimed the contract bill a law.

Owen could scarcely breathe. His father had always preached that the world was an unjust place, but somehow Owen had convinced himself that Olgard was an exception, a place where the ideals set forth by Trufic philosophers like Baron Dyrirnotic were destined to win the day over mankind's self-serving instincts. But no. After today, Olgard was no better than Tiderealm. Both were again slaver nations in principle, after all. Sure, one was a republic and one was a monarchy, but what was the point in being a republic if the power of representative government was used to persecute a minority of the people?

Arry dismissed the chamber for the midday break shortly after the vote. Sick at the thought of watching Tyus Redgrave and his compatriots celebrating yet another win, Owen hurried outside, desperate, like the day before, for a breath of fresh air.

He had scarcely exited the rotunda when he was accosted by a newspaper boy. "*The Daily Centichester,* sir?" the boy crowed, certain that he'd found a mark. "If you're in government, you'll want to have a look at this headline. That I can guarantee you."

Owen had nearly forgotten. He found a half-mark in his pocket, handed it over. The boy presented the paper's front cover with a flourish.

WALSH PROGENY HALTS MURDER
MASQUERADING AS A DUEL

LUCIEN GRINGER PULLS THE TRIGGER

No good deed goes unpunished, Owen thought, imagining the backlash this would cause. But it wasn't as if refusing to fight fire with fire would have helped. He had a target on his back now, no matter what he did.

Owen looked around. Others were trickling out, adjutants and senators alike, all eager for their midday ration of sun. The newspaper boy hurried after them, knowing that he had hot copy to peddle. Owen watched the boy make his rounds until he spotted a crop of dirty-blond hair in the customer mix. Tyus Redgrave bought a copy of the paper and digested the headline. The young senator's morning-long smile faded as he read the print, eyes sprinting left to right ever more furiously. Finished, the young lion jerked his head to the horizon, searching.

When he spotted Owen, he sneered and came storming.

"You'll have them retract this, Walsh, or you'll rue it! Do you hear me?"

Redgrave slapped the paper against his thigh as he approached, a makeshift war drum. Every person within hearing distance popped their heads up like chatter dogs, drawn to the sound of Redgrave's ire. Another spectacle in a day full of them.

Owen backed off the stone pavers that led into the Beacon, and onto an embankment of grass. Tyus pressed up on him like an aggressive rooster.

"These are honorable men, Walsh. They will not abide Baronite scum raking their names through the mud."

Owen jutted his chin out at the larger man. "My own name suffered a stain earlier this morning. Funny, I don't remember you voicing concern then."

Tyus leaned in. Handsome at a distance, up close he was all teeth and tobacco rot. "You've dug your own grave,

Walsh. I know these men. They won't suffer an insult like this. If I were you, I'd prepare my dueling pistol."

Owen's heart stuttered. His face blanched. Somehow the thought hadn't occurred to him.

Tyus saw that he had unnerved him. Flashing a grin, the young senator rolled up the newspaper and gave Owen a one-two tap on the shoulder. "I wonder if the half-breed and a Titan's strumpet will come along and rescue you during your duel, the way you rescued him? Seems unlikely, doesn't it?" And then he strolled away, content with the blow he had landed.

Owen didn't know what to do. Above him stood the many government men, watching in fascination. Even the Baronites couldn't help but gawk. He was a former president's son, a *fallen* president's son, and the vultures were circling.

He gave them all a long, cold stare. But he knew that he wasn't ready to walk the gauntlet. Besides, it would be another hour or so before the senate resumed business.

Time enough to get away for a bit.

Time enough to visit Charlsey Roges.

4

Two smaller versions of Gringold were standing guard outside Doc Bickerstaff's door when Owen arrived. Teenage toughs from the look of it, perhaps a couple years Owen's junior. *The daytime shift,* Owen thought. They straightened up when Owen approached, their faces blushing red.

"Is something the matter?" Owen asked when he saw then. He was genuinely perplexed.

"No, sir," answered the taller one, who had ears like cornstalks. "It's only...there's visitors, is all."

"Visitors?" Owen asked. But then he heard the voices coming from inside, dulcet tones of the female persuasion. "How long have they been here?"

"Not long," Cornstalk Ears replied, before quickly shaking his head. "That's not entirely true. The Harrish girl's been here for an hour or so, milling about. But she only went inside when the Torquecan woman arrived."

The Harrish girl? Owen wondered. But even as he began to speculate, he knew there was no point to it. He reached for the doorknob to Doc Bickerstaff's bright-red door, opened it, and went inside.

Charlsey Roges was sitting up at an angle in the makeshift bed Doc Bickerstaff had prepared for him in the main room, surrounded by women on both sides. One of the women, Owen intuited, was Charlsey's beloved, and the other...the other was the Titan's Daughter Owen had spoken to the night before in the temple, the same woman who had helped save Charlsey's life.

Emmaline.

The women stopped talking the moment he entered. They appraised him with welcoming eyes, but said nothing. Owen tried not to stare. He turned his attention to Charlsey and gave him a slight head nod.

"Mr. Roges, I hope you'll excuse the interruption. I had a break, and I thought I might stop by and check on your recovery."

Charlsey responded with a bright but pained smile. "Mr. Walsh, please, you are more than welcome here. Thank you for coming. I wish I could stand to greet you, to thank you…"

"Hush," the Torquecan woman said to Charlsey. "Save your energy." She turned to Owen. She was a shorter woman than Owen had imagined Charlsey's love interest would be, with large hips and an extraordinarily beautiful face. "He's not out of the woods yet. The bullet shattered his femur, and infection remains a real possibility. Not to mention that there are men who want him dead. Even if he survives, his days in Olgard are numbered."

Owen's first instinct was to protest, to insist that Charlsey could both regain his health and resume his old life. But the woman's blunt truth was too self-evident to contradict.

"You're the former president's son, are you not?" the Torquecan woman asked when it became clear that Owen wasn't going to respond.

"I am," he replied. It was a simple enough question to answer, and he was glad for it.

"Then you must aid us. It's the only way. We will leave for the Torquecan free state of Chineyaco as soon as Charlsey is able. I'll break my contract to Amelia Redgrave. I won't stay with her once she marries that monster Lucien

Gringer. You'll arrange it, you'll help us, you have powerful friends—"

"I—"

He was blessedly distracted by the appearance of Doc Bickerstaff in the back of the room, who entered with his pipe pursed tightly between his lips. An old scarecrow of a man who looked frail and withered at the best of times, Doc Bickerstaff appeared to have spent the last twenty-four hours engaged in negotiations with the grim reaper, discussing how to best expedite his exit from the planet.

Flustered by the Torquecan woman, Owen swung his attention to the doctor. "Doc Bickerstaff, thank you for—"

"You hear what she says in my house, Mr. Walsh," the old doctor interrupted, removing the pipe with one hand and raising a bony finger with the other. "It's bad enough I'm being guarded by the local riffraff while would-be murderers prowl my bushes, now there's a slave woman speaking of breaking the law beneath my very roof!"

"I am not a slave!" the Torquecan woman responded. "I am a contracted woman with a marriage offer from a true free man."

"Ha!" Doc Bickerstaff spat, spittle clinging to his chin. Owen was taken aback by the usually mild-mannered doctor's fit of pique. The doctor's hand was shaking so badly, it looked as if he might drop his pipe. "Shall you tell her, Mr. Walsh, or shall I?"

Owen didn't have the foggiest clue what Doc Bickerstaff was on about. He gave a befuddled little shrug of the shoulders.

"Of course you've nothing to say," the doctor said. He had an unhinged look. "Why would the son of the president who lost control of the country have any better sense of what's happening in Olgard than his father did?" Doc Bickerstaff turned to face the room. "Olgard is a Free Harrish country now. As Centichester is a Free Harrish city. Only a fool would fail to recognize it. So you go on believing that you're not a slave," he said, pointing to the Torquecan woman, "and you go on believing that the Baronites still hold sway in this town," he continued, now pointing his finger at Owen, "but as for me, I intend to face reality. I want this man out of my house before sundown. You tell Senator Stevens that, Mr. Walsh. I want him gone."

Owen searched for words, but, before he could find them, Doc Bickerstaff returned his pipe to his lips, wheeled around, and exited the room.

No one said a word, but the Torquecan woman began to cry, soundless tears that fell from her cheeks like a quiet but steady rain. Owen felt hot with emotion, though he wasn't sure if it was anger at Doc Bickerstaff or embarrassment at his impotence. How was he supposed to help? What was he supposed to do?

"I will do whatever it takes," he heard himself saying, his mouth suddenly standing up to his thoughts. "When Mr. Roges is recovered, I will help the two of you escape to Chineyaco, if that's what you desire. Contracts be damned." He was the only one in the room who knew that the contract laws had changed, but that seemed beside the point at the moment. The contract laws had been unjust before the day begun, and they were unjust now. For the first time in Owen's life, the business of government seemed worthy of nothing but his contempt.

"Thank you, Mr. Walsh," Charlsey said. "But where will I stay until I am recovered now that the doctor wants me gone?"

"Doc Bickerstaff isn't sending you anywhere," Owen replied. "I'll see to that."

Owen found the doctor in the back bedroom, going through the motion of sorting clothes. The doctor's wife had died two years ago, a loss that clung to the doctor at all times but perhaps exceptionally so when he tried his hand at domestic duties. Owen thought he looked like a rather befuddled specter, damned to spend the afterlife muddling through a chore he didn't comprehend.

"Doc Bickerstaff."

The old man sighed, dropped the shirt he was toying with, and turned to face Owen. His pipe jutted out of his mouth like a forgotten stage prop.

"Damned Baronites. Your lot couldn't hold on to power when it mattered. But Titan knows being powerless won't stop you from harassing an old man. Now be gone, boy," he said, waving Owen away with his hand. "And take the Torquecan with you."

Doc Bickerstaff *was* an old man. Owen could see that plainly enough. And he was scared. But it was no excuse for cowardice.

"I'll take Charlsey Roges off your hands as soon as possible," Owen said through gritted teeth. "But not until he's healthy enough to travel. Until then, he stays under your roof, and under your care. You owe the Baronite party...you owe my father...that much. In the meantime, we'll see to it that the extra protection you've had remains in place."

The doctor *harrumphed*. "This will be the end of me," he complained, overflowing with bitterness. "Like I said before, it's a Free Harrish town and a Free Harrish country now. Any man who associates with Baronites and Torquecans will soon find himself an outcast. At my age, I may as well start digging my grave."

"If you mean to die, you could at least try and do so with a little dignity," Owen snapped in reply. The doctor looked at Owen, eyes afire, but, unable to withstand the brilliance of Owen's own gaze, he looked away. Owen stared at the doctor a little longer, red hot with anger. The Baronite party, and William Walsh in particular, had elevated Doc Bickerstaff's station in Centichester beyond his wildest dreams. To gripe now that the political tides had turned was the height of ingratitude.

The doctor, undone by Owen's righteous glare, turned away and resumed the sad business of sorting his shirts.

Satisfied that he'd done all that he could do, Owen left the room.

"You're staying, for now. I'll start looking for a safe place for you to go once you're healthy enough to move. Until that time comes, there will be men stationed here for your protection. That's a promise."

Charlsey nodded, satisfied. His eyes were sunk back far in his head. He appeared to be in quite a bit of pain.

The Torquecan woman eyed Owen warily. "We have no choice but to believe you. So we will. But I may need your help before Charlsey does. I can't stay—"

Emmaline suddenly interrupted, her hand leaping to take hold of the Torquecan woman's. "Not here, Chitniza," she said, cutting her eyes to the back of the house. She leaned in and whispered in the Torquecan woman's ear. When the Torquecan woman nodded, Emmaline turned to Owen. "Mr. Walsh, I'm about to take my leave. Will you do me the favor of escorting me to my destination?"

Owen's heart leapt into his throat. The prehensile portion of his brain grasped at the obvious question— *Where are you going?*—but the love-struck side took quick control of his tongue, stammering out a "Y…Yes."

Emmaline gave—Chitniza, was it?—a quick hug and then stood to go. She strode by Owen without a word or a look, apparently expecting him to follow.

Which he did. Owen gave Charlsey and Chitniza an awkward bow of the head, and trailed Emmaline into the sunshine.

Together they sped by the two substitute Gringolds, who had been listening at the door. The two toughs mumbled apologies of some sort, but Owen couldn't slow down long enough to reply.

"I can't escort you if I can't keep up with you," Owen protested as Emmaline rounded onto the street, heading back in the direction of the Beacon. Doc Bickerstaff lived in the *lower half,* the area south of the government center where the professional classes lived. *Old Centichester,* some called it, although the affectation felt a little forced for a city so young. Owen kicked up little dust clouds as he hurried after Emmaline, navigating *Old Centichester's* rain-starved dirt roads.

Emmaline didn't slow down, and she didn't reply. For a brief moment, Owen wondered if she was running away from him. But then she ducked down a side road, and, when Owen followed, she pulled him behind the woodshed of an abandoned house.

"Chitniza needs a place to stay tonight," she announced with a hurried brashness. Seemingly apropos of nothing, her face colored red. "And so do I."

Owen sensed his own cheeks flaring. "Are you suggesting that the two of you stay with me?"

Emmaline gave him a perplexed look, as if she hadn't understood the question. Then she said, "If that's the only place, yes."

A dumb quiet descended. There were too many questions roiling in Owen's head for him to ask them all, and besides, he didn't know where to begin. But then it occurred to him that he could simply bypass the questions entirely, and give the answer that he wanted to give.

"Okay. You can stay with me. Chitniza too."

She paused to give him a look that he would have forwent his inheritance to capture in time. A look that said she had underestimated him; a look that bespoke an appreciation that she didn't know how to best convey.

"Thank you," she said at last.

"You're welcome."

They stood in silence for a moment, considering each other anew. Time slowed. The many problems currently plaguing Owen receded into the distance as the present moment expanded, becoming, somehow, life itself. Sunlight filtered through a canopy of tree leaves caught Emmaline's face in a fetching glow. For so long Owen's life had been a straight arrow shot from the bow of Walsh family expectations, but here and now, in Emmaline's presence, Owen saw that he didn't have to do what was expected of him. He could throw caution to the wind, he could risk everything, he could—

"Can we go there now?" Emmaline asked, breaking the trance. "I left the Titan's Daughters this morning, and I'm not exactly sure what will happen if someone from the temple recognizes me in the city."

He nodded solemnly. The afternoon session at the Beacon, and the matter of Wolfresh, and the likelihood that a challenge to a duel was in his near future, could wait.

"Again, thank you," she said. "After dusk, I'll send word to Chitniza. If need be, she'll come later tonight."

"How will you send word?" Owen asked.

She smiled at him faintly. A smile in lieu of an answer. "Shall we go?" she asked, the lilt in her voice pretending that she hadn't ignored his question.

"Of course," he replied. For the present moment, he could live with her sidestepping his questions. Especially now that he knew he had time to get at the mystery at the heart of the girl.

5

By the time he left Emmaline safely ensconced in the guest room of Mathias Potter's guest house, Owen was running nearly an hour late to the afternoon legislative session. The nipping guilt he felt for shirking his duties was starting to gnaw, so, to save time, he decided to walk the riverbank back to the Beacon rather than backtrack to the road. There was a wooden enclave that was tricky to traverse, but, familiar with the land, Owen followed a trail he had forged as an adventurous teenager, a fragmented here-and-again path that required a few leaps over narrow woodland ravines and one balancing act over a rotting snow elm that forded a tributary stream.

He was nearly out of the woods—his breeches and frock coat still impressively unsoiled—when he stepped on a clutch of wintersnake eggs in the undergrowth. Confused at first, he watched with a fascinated horror as two premature snakes emerged from the three eggs he had smashed. One slithered away as fast as it could, pausing once to strike at empty air. As it did, Owen got a clear look at the blue and white stripes that denoted its poisonous nature. The second snake hadn't fared as well as the first. Its body was broken, courtesy of Owen's shoe. It moved sporadically, spasmodically, a good quarter of its blue-and-white-striped body still stuck in the damaged egg. The third egg had taken the brunt of the blow. All that was left of it was a shattered mess of eggshell and snake matter.

Recovering from his surprise, Owen decided that the humane thing to do was to put the injured snake out of its misery. Careful not to miss his mark, Owen ground the heel of his shoe into the snake's head, severing it from the body. The snake, already broken, gave up the ghost without protest.

Unsettled by the encounter, Owen carefully walked the last few yards out of the woods, and continued on his way.

He sensed the doomful air the moment he entered the rotunda, as rich and pungent as a corpse flower.

Isaiah Braswell ran into the rotunda from the Pit and rushed by Owen without a word. The young adjutant's face was as white as a sheet. He gave Owen a glance that was equal parts judgement and confusion, but he didn't slow down.

Inside the Pit, a subdued half-moon of senators surrounded an empty desk. The senators and adjutants standing on the outskirts of the crescent were deathly quiet. Moving closer, Owen realized that a body was lying on the floor beside the desk. Owen walked down the aisle, knowing in his heart who was at the center.

As Owen had intuited, Senator Stevens was lying on the ground, his head propped up by Senator Thumb. The senator's right shoulder was rigid and raised. His hand was an eagle's talon. Drool dripped from the open slash of his mouth. He stared into the middle distance with wild white eyes.

"A massive stroke," someone said, perhaps for Owen's benefit.

The group resumed the uneasy business of waiting for the doctor to arrive.

Owen along with them.

Soon all the Stevenses were gathered in the Beacon. The senator's wife, Cornelia; the senator's daughter, Constance;

and the senator's son-in-law, Seth Templeton. They were the very picture of stoic Smoketon reserve as the doctor attended to the senator, all three standing in an orderly line awaiting the doctor's verdict.

At last, the doctor—not Doc Bickerstaff, but instead a Free Harrish physick with untamed black hair—stood and took Cornelia by the hand. The Baronite matriarch immediately withdrew her hand from the too-familiar doctor's, but otherwise stood as firm and silent as a rock. When the doctor was finished, she gave a little nod, and then there was a flurry of movement as several large men entered from the back carrying a stretcher, Gringold among them. The men assisted Jude Stevens into the stretcher.

It was one of the saddest sights Owen had ever seen. Jude Stevens, the greatest orator in the history of the Olgard nation and the staunchest defender of the Baronite philosophy this side of the Broken Ocean, being carried out of the Beacon on a stretcher. The senator stared dumbly into the beyond, his only sign of life the occasional undignified whimper. The Stevens family trailed behind him in a grim processional.

Owen didn't know what to do. He hadn't been present when the stroke had occurred, and now he was uncertain of his role. When Seth Templeton passed him by, Owen grabbed at the sleeve of Seth's tan waistcoat.

"Mr. Templeton."

It took Seth a moment to place Owen. "Mr. Walsh. You're here. Why weren't you the one to contact the family? Mr. Braswell—"

"I know. I apologize. I wasn't in the chamber at the time." The Pit was pin-drop silent. Every ear in the place was attuned to the exchange. "Let me come with you. Surely I can be of some assistance."

"There's nothing to be done now." Templeton's words sounded like an indictment of Owen's absence, regardless of whether he meant it that way. Seth glanced over his shoulder at the departing processional. "Perhaps tomorrow. After the family has had a little time to recover."

Owen nodded. Seth, however, didn't see him. He was already pulling away to leave.

Up ahead, Gringold opened the oak doors leading to the rotunda with the broad of his back, keeping steady hold of the front of the stretcher with his massive arms. Along with the two men holding up the back of the stretcher, Gringold carried the legendary Senator Jude Stevens out of the Beacon for the last time.

Owen was at a loss. He went and sat on the wooden benches reserved for the adjutants when the senate was in session, and put his head in his hands.

For the longest time, no one approached. Only when Arry called the senate back into session did someone sit beside him.

"Where were you?" the someone whispered.

Owen looked up. Sitting beside him was the all-too-earnest Isaiah Braswell, adjutant to Senator Thumb. Isaiah was six years Owen's senior, but often exhibited the innocence and intensity of feeling of a younger man. Emphasizing this impression was the fact that Isaiah had a face so boyish, he might have been mistaken for a page to the Titan's merciful aspect. Which, of course, he had once been.

"It doesn't matter now," Owen replied.

Up on the dais, the vice president was rambling. Arry was making the case that the day's session should be brought to a close, interspersing his comments with praise for the stricken Stevens. Owen was inclined to agree, but something was off about Rufus Arry's delivery: the vice president sounded uncharacteristically nervous and defensive. Owen stole a look at *Long Stache* (the nickname given to the VP in both the Baronite and Free Harrish press). He looked like a rural priest who had lost faith in the middle of his sermon and could see Cairth's hellhounds from the Bottom Black closing in.

Isaiah leaned in for a second tête-à-tête.

"Their caucus is fractured, but after this morning, it's impossible to tell who's with who. When the afternoon session commenced, Redgrave puffed up like a peacock and proposed invading Wolfresh. With Arry's backing, I believe. His speech was full of the usual fearmongering about a new Deer King. But not a single Free Harrish said a word in support, and once they started tallying the votes, the numbers didn't fall Redgrave's way. It was during the vote that Senator Stevens…collapsed. Now Arry wants to save face and delay the rest of the vote until tomorrow. But I don't think Shroud's going to let him off the hook. He's sending Tyus and the vice president a message, and he means to send it today."

Owen tried to process this strange development, but his mind was clouded with the memory of the half-paralyzed Stevens. Besides, whatever was happening, Briggs Shroud was the puppet master pulling the strings. And he was no friend to the Baronite cause.

"It's unfortunate we can't capitalize," Isaiah continued. "But there's not an angle. I can't imagine a single Baronite who would vote for invading Wolfresh. Perhaps Senator Whitestone, if Shroud told him to. Although I suppose Whitestone is no longer a Baronite after this morning." Isaiah paused. "Titan only knows if Shroud has gotten to others."

Owen let his gaze wander to the smallest man in the chamber, the aforementioned senate majority leader. Briggs Shroud was a titan in his own right, no matter how miniscule his size; he had been a key player in Olgardian politics since the Sovereignty War. Universally credited with being the chief architect of the Olgard constitution (along with Baronite-in-exile Napoleon Wright), Shroud had tied his political fortunes to the mast of the frigate Randolph near two decades prior, and was now reaping the rewards. Looking at the shrewd little man from across the room, Owen knew the answer to Isaiah's postulation.

"He's gotten to as many of ours as was necessary, I'm sure," Owen said darkly, before resuming his quiet.

Up on the dais, Arry finished his desperate and impassioned spiel. Then, looking anxiously at the senate, he called for a voice vote to bring the session to an end.

There wasn't a single "aye." None from the Baronites. None from the Free Harrish. Even Tyus Redgrave kept his mouth shut, although he appeared to be grinding stones between his teeth in his effort to do so.

Owen turned his attention once more to Briggs Shroud, who was staring at Rufus Arry with a look of vengeful contempt. Twice today the Free Harrish caucus had threatened to undercut Shroud's authority, and twice the stern little taskmaster had set his caucus to rights. Whatever secret war was being waged for power among the majority, Shroud had won.

Shroud kept staring at Arry, parading his victory without saying a word. A deep fire had settled in the little man's eyes, the hypnotic flame of triumph. Owen was watching him when, for a brief moment, the flame burst into a roaring conflagration, and out of the corner of Shroud's mouth what looked like a drop of blood appeared. But in the same instance the senator's tongue darted and stole the blood away, and the flame vanished. The Senator's frostbitten blue eyes quickly returned, and his hair, always a downy snow-white, reassumed its natural hue.

Owen was confused. Had he hallucinated? In retrospect, it seemed that Shroud's eyes hadn't been a flame so much as a roaring sun, only instead of orange, the irises had been a deep and pulsing red. And Shroud's hair? Had it changed color too? It had all happened so fast, but Owen could have sworn that Shroud's famously lax and alabaster mane had crackled with color, if only for a moment. And had that really been a drop of blood trembling on the corner of the senator's lips, before he licked it away?

"Mr. Vice President," Briggs Shroud spoke, interrupting Owen's befuddled musings, "the voice vote has failed. If you would now resume recording the vote on the Wolfresh proposition, I can assure you that once the vote is finished, we will adjourn the remainder of the day's session out of respect for Senator Stevens."

Arry had the look of a long and limp noodle, one left to perish on the plate. Moustache quivering, he resumed the roll call cut short by Senator Stevens's stroke.

Nays poured out of ready mouths.

As the votes were being recorded, Owen kept his eyes on Shroud, hoping to catch a repeat performance of the senator's earlier transmutation. But the senator had settled back into his customary form, that of a tiny wielder of vast power. Briggs Shroud sat on his desk chair, letting the last act of the day's script play out, exactly as he had written it.

Owen gave up. Whatever he had seen, he wasn't going to see it again. Not today, at least.

Looking away at last, Owen sensed that he was being stared at. Scanning the Free Harrish contingent, he quickly found the source. While he had been looking at Shroud, Tyus Redgrave had been looking at him.

The young senator's gaze was a malicious one.

The session was adjourned.

Time sped up. Owen's heart thump-thumped as he left the Pit. Braswell walked alongside him, matching him stride for stride, without saying a word. When they entered the rotunda, its ministerial glory rang hollow. Norman Burgod stood on his plinth beside the doorway, but he was lost in his own troubles as always, and had no words of wisdom for Owen.

Tyus Redgrave stalked, an injured lion on the prowl.

Outside, the sky was dizzyingly blue. It was warm for winter, the sun aggressive even at its seasonal slant. Disoriented, Owen started west across the stone pavers, but then veered north, looking a little like a drunk. He was at the front of a pack, but the wolves behind him were onlookers and enemies, not allies. He scanned his surroundings, hoping to see what was coming.

Off in the distance, the Marinus River roared.

Then he saw them. They were approaching from the southwest, climbing up the embankment that led to the Beacon. A duo: the bullfrog, Lucien Gringer, flanked by a man with a stiff brown moustache and pursed lips. Lanky scarecrow Duncan Broggs was nowhere to be seen. Owen searched for the name Charlsey had given him. *Jeremiah Luck urged me to pull the trigger. But before I could, he jerked my hand to the sky and pulled the trigger for me.* Jeremiah Luck. The man who had fled the scene. But now that the story had run in *The Daily Centichester* and his honor was on the line, Jeremiah was forced to show his face in the light of day.

And there was only one way for a man to defend his honor in Olgard.

Owen came to a stop. His foes descended like a murder of crows.

"Owen Walsh!?" Lucien Gringer barked.

Jeremiah Luck cut questioning hazel-brown eyes at Lucien. Gringer, with something of a huff, gave way and allowed Luck to take the lead. Owen and Jeremiah squared off, schoolyard style.

Lucien stood to Jeremiah's left, looking every bit the eager bruiser. Owen wondered if they'd drawn lots to determine who had the honor.

Tyus Redgrave rounded into view and took up position on Jeremiah's right. There was a dark and terrible rage in his eyes. He had been spanked in the senate, but this was a different setting. Out here he could dabble vicariously in violence. Out here he could take his revenge on a world that didn't always submit to his will.

To Owen's left, Isaiah Braswell. *There's one true Baronite remaining, at least,* Owen thought.

Jeremiah spoke. His voice was gussied up in bravado. "Mr. Walsh, a story ran today in *The Daily Centichester* that maligned my reputation. I have reason to believe that you are the source for this story. Do you deny it?"

Owen channeled the Walsh spirit, best characterized by a blood that could boil on demand. He spat his reply with venom. "I take it you are referring to the story that pinpointed Jeremiah Luck as the scoundrel who fled the field of the Gringer-Roges duel after disingenuously posing as Roges's second? The story that outlined in detail Jeremiah Luck's efforts to assist in the murder of the ambushed principal?!"

Jeremiah bunched up his gritted teeth under the canopy of his moustache. "*I* am Jeremiah Luck, sir. And yes, that is the story, though its contents have no basis in truth. Now, answer me. Are you the source?"

"I am. And if that answer doesn't suffice, I'll be glad to explain in detail to everyone here how you—" Owen pointed at Jeremiah, "—and you—" Owen pointed at Lucien Gringer, "—staged a duel for the purpose of murdering Charlsey Roges." He turned his gaze on Redgrave. "At your behest, no doubt. That's right. I know the truth of the matter, the motivation behind the killing. That part might not have run in the newspaper, but I'm no less certain that it's true."

Owen's words hung suspended in the air for a long minute as his antagonists assessed the weight of them. Tyus reached his conclusion first. "You've overplayed your hand, Walsh," he said coolly, the bunched-up anger on his face suddenly dissipating. "You defend Torquecan rapists, you contrive outlandish tales, and you sully the honor of good Titan-worshipping Harrish men. But the day of your reckoning is upon you. Like all Baronites, your time is over."

Tyus receded, taking a half step back. Jeremiah stepped forward and jutted his chin out at Owen. "You have left me no choice. I challenge you to a duel."

If there was another option, Owen didn't see it. "I accept," he said.

Lucien Gringer stepped forward. He jabbed a stubby finger in Owen's chest. "I too challenge you to a duel," he growled.

"As do I," chimed in Tyus Redgrave. Owen's ability to process what was occurring was being swept away on a tide of disbelief. Had he just been challenged to three separate duels? All at once he felt like the famed Ithiaian emperor Claius Caya, the knives coming at him from all sides. He stared at Redgrave with a stunned expression. Tyus gave him a sanguine smile in turn, his cheeks ruddy with restrained bloodlust. "I propose every subsequent Porchen until the matter is resolved. Jeremiah is a crack shot, so one Wednesday will likely suffice. Who will serve as your second, Walsh? This adjutant?"

Owen could scarcely hear Tyus for the bedlam in his brain.

"I will gladly serve as your second," Braswell said to Owen from what seemed like a great distance. "If it please you."

Owen managed to bob his head up and down. *I'm a dead man,* he thought. He forced himself to look at his adversaries. Two days ago the scoundrels before him had conspired to murder Charlsey Roges under the guise of a duel. Now Owen had agreed to duel each of them separately. A trap had been set, and he had walked right into it. All that was left for Owen to do now was die.

The arrangements were made. Since Owen couldn't talk, Isaiah Braswell served as his mouthpiece. The competent adjutant took to his new role as a second with a self-assuredness that made Owen feel paranoid. *Was this part of the setup?* He knew in his heart that it wasn't, but he had never felt so vulnerable, so exposed.

"Wandering Bluff. Next Porchen, at dawn," Tyus Redgrave announced when the matter was settled. At some point during the negotiations, Tyus had claimed the role of Luck's second. Owen assumed it was because he wanted a good vantage point to witness the coup de grace.

And then it was over. Owen's three would-be killers gave him satisfied smirks, turned, and walked away. Isaiah shook Owen's hand, and said something about how the Bronze Titan protects honest men. Then he left. Owen, however, didn't move. For the longest time he simply stood in silence on the stone pavers, trying to remember what his life had been like only minutes earlier, when he hadn't been a man destined to die.

While he was walking home, the temperature dropped with the sun. The season of winter, remembering. Owen drew his frock coat fast around his shoulders and carried on.

As Owen drew close to the guest house, he glanced at the red-roofed, white wood-paneled mansion eighty yards further on. The Potter house, better known as the Dove Roost. He hoped to catch sight of Mathias Potter standing out in the yard, or perhaps sitting on the massive wraparound porch. If there was ever a day that he could use advice from the twin brother of the patriarch of the Baronite Party, it was today. But, as usual, Mathias Potter was nowhere to be seen.

It's for the better, he thought, remembering his guest. Once inside, he stood quietly and listened for the creak of floorboards upstairs. Despite the pressing matter of three imminent duels, his young man's mind couldn't help but be distracted by the girl in the house. He even felt a little excited at the prospect of sharing his news with her. But, after a moment's waiting, there was no sound of corresponding movement to match the ones made by his arrival.

"Emmaline?" he called out.

No reply. Then he remembered what she had told him. *After dusk, I'll send word to Chitniza.*

Outside, the sun was still up, though it sat wan and weak in the sky. *She sent word early,* he surmised. But it was just a guess. He had no real clue as to the mysterious workings of Emmaline's mind.

He decided to go for a short walk. He thought there was a chance that he might find her outside. He took his favorite route down to the river, through a grove of sycamores that led to a little rock beach. Once on the beach, he fell into a deep silence. He stood still, trying not to think. Behind him, the sun worked its way into its daily grave. He continued meditating until the daylight candle was snuffed. Then he made his way back home.

Inside, he went about his evening chores. He started a fire. Once the flame had settled into the wood, he made supper, two eggs in a skillet and a side of salted pork, washed down with a tankard of cider. He thought the stress of the day might interfere with his stomach settling, but to his surprise the eggs and pork went down easy. He was famished, and, stressed or not, his digestive tract made short work of what it was offered.

Refreshed, he took a long look at the pinewood desk in the corner of the room, where the quill and ink sat patiently waiting. He needed to write his father, both about the duels and Jude Stevens's stroke. In his mind's eye he tried to summon an image of how his father would react when he read the news, but the image he conjured was a blurry one, less a vision of William Walsh than an imagining of a distraught deity, the god of paternal grief. He realized, with a touch of panic, that he couldn't envision his father's face clearly. Then he realized, with a touch of fright, that he might never see his father's face again.

Owen felt something giving way inside of him when the door opened. He turned and there she stood. Emmaline. The Titan's Daughter. The Stoneman's daughter. Though from looking at her, it appeared she was now neither. Her father was dead, and she no longer wore the black and white robes of a daughter of the Bronze Titan. Instead, she wore a slim buckskin dress. Owen was unsettled by the sight of it. She looked like a native. Like a Massaporan. But if he was discomfited, she was the opposite, at once at ease in her clothing and intense in her manner. He found her eyes. She was looking at him like she had a knife on her tongue, and was deciding whether or not to use it.

"What is it?" he asked. Suddenly his three duels were the most insignificant matter on the planet.

She cut him to the quick. "Charlsey Roges is dead."

6

Owen dreamed bloody, straightforward dreams. Doc Bickerstaff sawing away at Charlsey's leg, muttering about an infection, murder in his movements. Chitniza swearing off absconding to Chineyaco, swearing off help from hapless presidents' sons, swearing revenge. Luck, the bullfrog, and the lordly lion all wielding pistols, singing a song about death on a rise of land overlooking the river. Emmaline, inscrutable. Owen's father and mother reading a letter together, and weeping.

It was as if Owen's mind was so overwhelmed by the blunt realities of his life that it had forgotten how to stir his fears into a subconscious soup.

But surprisingly, when he awoke, he felt a sense of peace. He had always had a fatalistic sensibility, and now that death was in the cards, he couldn't help but think that it made a certain sense. His father's presidency was over. Jude Stevens had been disabled by a stroke. The Baronite party was in complete disarray. It only seemed logical that one last, summative tragedy should befall the Baronite orthodoxy, and what better grace note could there be than for the blueblood heir to the Baronite legacy to meet an early and untimely death?

He was readying himself for work when it dawned on him that he no longer had an official capacity in the government. While chewing on this realization, Emmaline came down the stairs, wearing the same buckskin dress as the night before.

Their conversation the previous evening had been a short one. She had filled him in on the details of Charlsey's death and Chitniza's change of plans, and then she had retired. Now she looked at him with uncertain eyes, and he realized, for the first time, that she likely felt as unsteady around him as he did around her.

"Good morning," he said.

"Good morning," she replied.

He knew there was no sense in waiting to tell her. "Yesterday I was challenged to a duel by three different men. The first engagement is next Porchen."

She held his gaze with a soft stare, but she said nothing.

Owen continued. "In addition, Senator Stevens, the man I work for, suffered a stroke. He'll never work again. Compounding that with the duels, I'm at a bit of a loss as to what to do today."

"You could explain to me why three men challenged you to a duel while you showed me around the estate," she said.

The thought of showing Emmaline around the Potter grounds sounded lovely. But he also knew that it was a foolish one. "I would enjoy nothing more. But I don't think it would be wise. Mathias Potter is a good and reasonable man, but if he discovered that I was hosting a female in the guest house, and a runaway from the Titan's Daughters, no less, I imagine we'd both soon find ourselves without a place to live."

Emmaline gave her hair a gentle toss, and offered Owen a smile that bordered on cheeky. "Are you sure?" she asked. "When I spoke to him yesterday, he implied that I was welcome for as long as was necessary."

A spit-gob of disbelief lodged in Owen's throat, and he had to cough it out. "That can't be true. You spoke to Mathias Potter? How in the name of the Bronze Titan—"

"He saw you smuggling me in from one of the windows in...I think he called it the Dove Roost? After you left, he walked down and made his introductions. He's a kind man. Wise too. Wishes you would come up and chat more often. We reached an understanding of sorts. He's resolved to see no evil concerning my stay, so to speak. So there's no need for the two of us to skulk around fearing that we'll be found out."

Owen could hardly believe it. Mathias Potter was an infirm old man who could barely summon the energy to sit for long spells on his porch. What youthful demon had possessed him to walk all the way down to the guest house to speak to Emmaline? And to suggest that he had okayed Emmaline staying with Owen unchaperoned? If that was true—and Owen highly doubted that it was—then Owen was almost disappointed in Mathias Potter. Here Owen had finally risked his sterling reputation as a president's son, and the adult in charge didn't even care.

"That doesn't seem—"

"We can go speak to him together if you like?" Emmaline interrupted. "Although I would imagine he's still sleeping at this hour. Perhaps we could take a walk around the estate together first."

Owen decided to stop looking a gift horse in the mouth. "Yes. Let's do that. Let's go for a walk." He looked at the loaf of bread on the table. "But first, let's have breakfast."

They walked, and they talked. The walking was the easy part. At first Owen was uncomfortable with the many lingering silences between them. He was a Walsh, and Walshes talked; when Walshes weren't talking, they were thinking of something to say. But Emmaline treated the silences as if they were of equal value to conversation; she seemed in no hurry whatsoever to resume their dialogue when it broke down. After a bit, Owen began to relax into the intervals of quiet. Not only was the silence peaceful, it was also latent with the promise of what they might share with one another next.

Throughout, Owen led the tour around the estate. The Potter estate was unlike the other estates surrounding Centichester. In the classic Harrish sense, it wasn't an estate at all. Where once acres upon acres of cultivated farmland greeted those approaching the house, now a wild and scraggly mess of thickets and tall grasses lined the wide dirt drive. A forest in rebirth. Closer to the houses, wide plains of clover ruled the day. The clover funneled into a mighty V that rolled down, down, down to the Marinus River, but off to the sides of the weed grass (both to the north and to the south) stood trees that had never known the axe: great, water-greedy sycamores, spindly mush willows, dancing birch, and dozens more.

They were walking the southern woods—perhaps a quarter mile from the spot where Owen had stepped on the wintersnake eggs the previous day—when, to his surprise, Emmaline asked him about the duels.

"The duels are connected to Charlsey Roges, aren't they?"

Owen nodded. Now that he had tasted Emmaline's sweet silences, he was loath to stuff his mouth with words.

"They'll kill you, if they can," Emmaline said with a gentle matter-of-factness. "Killing is how they win."

"I don't want to duel," Owen said. "So how do I win?"

"That's simple," she replied. "You stay alive."

Owen laughed bitterly. "That's easy for you to say. You're a woman. Men in Olgard who refuse to duel may as well retire from public life. And you're forgetting that my father was the president. I have a legacy to uphold. I'd rather die than have it seem that I wasn't willing to stand up for my beliefs."

Owen immediately regretted his outburst. His intention hadn't been to lash out at Emmaline, but, given the chance to speak his anxieties over the duels into existence, that was what he'd done. He cast a timorous glance her way. She didn't look off-put. Rather, she stared at him with pensive green-brown eyes, somehow giving the impression that she was both thinking about him and not thinking about him at all.

"I didn't say not to duel," she replied. "I said not to die. I've thrice been the captive of people that I thought were going to kill me. A couple of times I tried killing them first, but that never worked out. So instead I focused on staying alive. Though it wasn't always clear how to do so, the way always presented itself in the end."

Owen was too flabbergasted to respond. He looked at Emmaline. Her face was the same blunt instrument of honesty that it always was. Outlandish or not, he believed her.

They began backtracking to the house. Yet another silence descended. Unlike with the other silences, Owen struggled to stay present this time. His mind kept slipping into the vortex of his troubles.

He was spiraling into the chasm when he felt a hand take hold of his own. Emmaline. He looked down at her hand, then he looked at her. But for some reason she wouldn't look at him. She had cast a spell, perhaps on herself, and it seemed looking at him might undo the magic.

Owen felt a lightness overcome his being. He decided that although she couldn't look at him, nothing was stopping him from looking at her. He stole glance after glance after glance, soaking in everything about her. She was beautiful in an untamed sort of way, which wasn't to say that she was wild, only that convention had eluded her at some point, and it was clear there was no going back to find it. She was sleek and white-cheeked and brown-haired and green-eyed and bold enough to take hold of the hand of a president's son and sufficiently shy to avert her eyes and strangely clad in a buckskin dress and, Titan forgive him, he was certain that he loved her.

They emerged from the woods back onto the plain of clover. Emmaline nodded north. Owen followed her gaze. Far away, on the front porch of the Dove Roost, sat the old man. Mathias Potter.

Emmaline dropped his hand. "You should go and speak to him," she said. "I'll wait for you at the house."

The old joke about the Potter brothers was that Brigand Potter had a face you couldn't forget, whereas Mathias had one you couldn't remember. More than once Owen had heard his father say that the reason the joke was funny was because it had a touch of truth to it. Brigand Potter had died by the time Owen was born, so Owen could only pass judgment on the more forgettable of the identical twins. Based on what he'd seen, he had to agree. Mathias looked like a prosaic mishmash of every old man Owen had ever met.

Mathias was sitting on a rocking chair, facing in Owen's direction as Owen climbed the gentle rise to the Dove Roost. He didn't wave or speak or acknowledge Owen's approach in any way. It wasn't until Owen was upon him that he realized why.

The old man's eyes were closed.

Owen stood at a loss for a moment on the other side of the paint-chipped porch railing, uncertain what to do. It crossed his mind that Mathias might be dead. But then, as if awakening from a gentle dream, the old man slowly opened his eyes. He appeared entirely unsurprised by Owen's presence.

"Mr. Walsh."

Owen nodded, and gave a slight bow. "Mr. Potter," he responded. Mathias Potter had only been a bit political player during his day, but he was the brother of the man who had spurred Olgard toward Baronism. For that reason alone, he was a god in Owen's eyes.

"You've had an eventful few days."

Owen didn't know how to reply. Did Mathias know about Jude Stevens? Did he how know about the duels? Or was he simply referring to Emmaline?

"Yes, sir," he responded. "What have you heard?"

Mathias grinned, exposing an impressive set of dentures. Rumor had it that the ivory in his teeth had crossed over before the Sundering. "Gabriella is inside," Mathias said, referring to his niece and daytime caretaker. "She told me about Jude's stroke this morning. And she told me about your duels. You have three on tap, correct? Seems a bit much, but perhaps you've said your prayers to the Titan's formidable aspect. What else? Ah, yes. I spoke to your house guest yesterday evening. So I know about her. But by all means, Mr. Walsh, if there's more, I'm all ears."

Owen's cheeks colored. "No, Mr. Potter. That's it."

Mathias gave a little chuckle. Then he motioned to the empty rocking chair to his left. "Join me on the porch, will you? I'm an old man, and my hearing isn't what it used to be."

"Of course."

The porch railing wrapped around the front of the house, leaving Owen with no choice but to walk until he was out of sight before stepping up onto the porch and doubling back. Nearly a minute passed before he took his seat.

"Good, good," Mathias said once Owen was seated, patting his hand on the arm of the rocker. The old fellow was livelier than Owen had ever seen him. "What can I do for you this morning? You've come to ask my permission about the Stoneman's daughter after the fact, perhaps?"

Owen's embarrassment was trumped only by his surprise that Mathias knew about Emmaline's background. "My apologies, sir. But I had to make a split-second decision yesterday. One that I thought was in Emmaline's best interests. So I made it."

Mathias gave the armrest a little slap. "And you made the right one. The girl is in a bit of a bind. You have that in common, I suppose. When two people are trapped in a corner, the least they can do is have each other's back."

All this talk about Emmaline was making Owen feel uncomfortable. "Yes sir," he replied. He considered thanking Mathias for allowing Emmaline to stay, but decided not to emphasize the subject. "Sir," he said, leaning far enough forward in the rocker that all motion stopped,

"I wondered if you had any advice for me. With Senator Stevens gone, the Baronite Party is doomed. Likely we were doomed already, but now the loss is complete. And they mean to kill me, sir. Just like they killed Charlsey Roges."

"The Torquecan?"

"Yes, sir. He was half-Torquecan, but yes. They wanted him dead, and now he's dead. And I'm next. What they really want is to kill Baronism, to rid Olgard of Baron Dyrirnotic's ideals, and damned if they're not nearly to their goal." He realized he had just profaned in front of Mathias Potter, but it didn't stop him. Now that he was finally venting, it felt good to get it off his chest. "The Free Harrish have undermined Olgard from the very beginning. They're base men, the lot of them. Murderers, cheats, slavers, and cowards. They destroyed my father's presidency with claims of monarchism, and they made common cause with the slavers in Tiderealm. Now they're dividing and conquering the Baronites that remain. Or they're challenging them to duels." He put his head in his hands. "Please, Mr. Potter. Help me. What would you do if you were in my position? What would your brother have done?"

"My brother—" Mathias began, then broke off in a strange, high-pitched laugh. Startled, Owen jerked his head out of his hands, quick enough to catch sight of an odd flash of green crossing the old man's eyes. Mathias continued his story as if nothing out of the ordinary had happened. "—was a true believer in Baronism. Separation of powers. Natural rights. The whole deal. He caught the Trufic philosopher's disease like it was the damn plague. And our family aristocratic. Titan forgive us. The Penroses and the Wheskers wouldn't, that's for certain. But by the end, even Brigand understood that Baronism would one day fall. Or it would be corrupted. It's mankind's plight, is it not? To try and fashion utopias only to watch them crumble to dust before our very eyes? They never last. And so the same will happen to Baronism."

Owen was stunned. He kept waiting for Mathias to continue his thought, but instead the old man accelerated his rocking, and set his jaw to chewing air.

"That's it?" Owen asked at last, when he could take it no more. The Walsh in him wanted to scream. "Baronism will fall? All hope is lost? We should simply accept our fate, and surrender? Accept our fate and die?"

Mathias laughed yet again, and, as he did, Owen thought he saw a strange green shadow traverse the horizon of his pupils. "We all die, my boy! Nothing to be scared of there. But we can live again. And often do. Take my woods, for example."

Hesitantly, Owen turned to stare at the mighty forest down by the river. Mathias redirected him. "Not those woods. My fledgling forest. Where the fields used to be."

Owen leaned forward and craned his neck over the porch railing. The unsightly jumble of weeds, tall grasses, and yes, what appeared to be the beginnings of a few small trees jostled over what had once been the finest farmland in all of Centichester.

Mathias continued. "I was a boy when my grandfather first cleared the land. Acres upon acres of old-growth forest, gone forever. I cried. Not my brother, though. Brigand laughed at me. Told me it was in the natural order of things. 'The Titan says in the *Superior Scrolls* that man should work the land, and make bread.' Ha! Funny how my brother had changed his tune by the end."

Owen was a little befuddled by the turn the conversation had taken. How had they gotten to forests? All the same, he felt obliged to ask the obvious question. "Why did he change his tune? What happened?"

"He looked into the eyes of a god."

A chill went up Owen's spine. "The—the Deer King?"

Mathias smacked his sandpapery mouth, curled his lips at the corners. "The *Dachahelu*, yes. Killing the Massaporan god changed Brigand. Before he died, he told me 'Turn the land back over to the forests, Mathias.' And so I have."

Tendrils of unease stroked Owen's nervous system. Difficult as it was for him to believe, it sounded like Mathias Potter was speaking fondly of the Massaporans' demonic deity.

"Think whatever you want of me, son," Mathias said, as if reading his mind. "I'm too old to care."

Owen did just that. He thought a million thoughts, without saying a single word.

Mathias sighed. "I know—you require a different sort of advice from me, advice that will help you stay alive and persist with politics. Here it is, then. First, do what it takes to survive your duels. Then, do your best to infect the Free Harrish ideology with the old Baronite strain. The time and place will present itself sooner than you'd think, I'm sure. Right now the Free Harrish are remaking the world, but come tomorrow their ideas will crumble under the weight of human folly. You being a Walsh, I'm certain you can position yourself to take advantage when it does."

It wasn't much in the way of advice, but Owen decided that it was the best Mathias Potter was going to offer. "Thank you, Mr. Potter," he said.

It had been a strange and surreal conversation, and now Owen desperately wanted to leave. He looked across the declining field of clover toward the guest house. He wanted to go there now. To spend what time he had left before the duel soaking up the sweet silences the girl inside had to offer.

"You may take your leave, Mr. Walsh," Mathias said, reading his mind once again.

And so he did.

When he returned, Emmaline wasn't there. After looking and calling for her, he elected to believe that she had gone out for yet another walk.

He thought for a moment that he might have a little time to kill, until the pinewood desk in the corner drew his eye. He sighed. *No better time than the present,* he thought. He walked over to the desk, sat down, and dipped his quill in the inkpot. By the light of the bountiful summer sun pouring in through the window, he wrote his father a letter.

Dear Father,

I have been challenged to three duels. My apologies for stating the blunt truth of the matter at the outset, but I could think of no way to temper the blow. I intervened to stop the murder of a Torquecan man who has subsequently died, and now the offended parties desire their recompense. Tyus Redgrave numbers among them. The Torquecan was formerly contracted to the Redgrave family, and I have reason to believe that the late secretary of state was the murdered man's father. But I digress. The first of the duels is Porchen next against a man named Jeremiah Luck. Likely you will have read this letter by then, though without sufficient time to reach me with a reply.

Also, Senator Stevens had a stroke. And the Free Harrish have passed a law permitting lifetime contracts, in effect reinstituting slavery. Baronism fails to exist in any meaningful way.

Blunt truths, father. We Walshes are unsparing men. Forgive me if I remind you too much of yourself.

Give mother and Abigail my love. If I survive the first duel, I will read your return letter with a great hunger. If I do not survive, know that I went to my grave defending the ideals you taught me to believe in.

Your obedient son,

Owen

Finished, he sealed the letter in an envelope. It being Prayden, the last day of the work week, Owen knew that if he didn't send the letter today, his father might not hear news of the duel until it was over. Or worse (and more likely), William Walsh would hear the news from someone else. Undoubtedly other quills in the capital had already taken up the task of informing the second president of Olgard that his only son might perish Porchen next.

He called out for Emmaline one last time, speaking loud enough that she would surely hear him. There was no reply. He tried his name out on her tongue once more, sounding a lovesick note. Some desperate, animal part of him wanted to continue repeating her name, but, for fear of losing all sense of propriety (and for fear that she might somehow hear him) he refrained from doing so.

He sighed.

Envelope in hand, he left the house, ready to walk into town.

Seford's Place had long been the Centichester den where politicos of the Baronite persuasion gathered, so it was there that Owen went. He had no real desire to interact with fellow members of his party, but Seford's was one of the few inns and pubs that riders traveling north and south stopped to frequent, knowing that a mark might be made carrying correspondence to and fro.

The midday crowd was larger than Owen had expected. Nearly every table in the front room was full. At a table in the back corner, a clot of men had formed, and were conversing in what appeared to be a conspiratorial fashion. Owen glanced at the men. Unable to discern their respective identities, he took a longer look, going against the pledge he had made to himself to be as inconspicuous as possible. The lack of light in the corner of the room smudged the men's appearances, but, as Owen continued to stare, the devil in the center of the dark knot revealed his true form.

Napoleon Wright. The Baronite (supposedly) in exile.

What in Cairth's cracked teeth is he doing here? Owen thought. Napoleon had left the capital in disgrace at the start of William Walsh's presidency, not for definitive proof of any specific wrongdoing, but because of two persistent rumors. One: he was having an affair with his wife's sister. And two: he was an actual monarchist (as opposed to the many Baronites who were unjustly accused by the Free Harrish of being monarchists). Because Napoleon was Norman Burgod's protégé, his political brethren had turned a blind eye to the secretary of the treasury's foibles during the Burgod presidency, but when Walsh took charge, Napoleon's enemies pounced. William Walsh among them. Napoleon had spent his years in exile living on the Tiderealm border, purportedly nurturing his contacts within the Whesker kingdom.

And now, he had returned.

Owen redirected his attention to the bar. Snowy Sam Girt—so named because of his whiter-than-white beard—stood behind the counter with a pitcher of cider. Owen approached Sam, knowing that he was the man who knew how to get a letter to its proper destination.

"Sam," he said, reaching into his coat and pulling out the letter as he approached, "I need you to get this to my father."

Sam, who had never mastered the art of concealing his emotions, gave Owen a look reserved for the damned. "Sure, Mr. Walsh. I know of a couple riders who will be coming through later today. I'll give yours to the most trustworthy one."

Owen slid two marks across the counter. "Thank you, Sam."

Sam took the two marks, but as he did, his eyes drifted behind Owen. Someone was approaching. "I thought it would be a cold day in the Black Bottom before..." Sam murmured, but his voice drifted off and he turned away with Owen's letter and the money, leaving to complete some bogus business at the opposite end of the bar.

Owen turned. Napoleon Wright stood facing him. Owen's memories of the former secretary of the treasury were more his father's than his own, but even so, he would have recognized Napoleon anywhere. *The reason he can sell Cairth's ideas is because he possesses the Titan's own face,* William Walsh had oft complained of Burgod's right-hand man, and Owen was compelled to agree. Looking at Napoleon was like looking at Trufic paintings of old Ithiaian demigods.

"Mr. Walsh." Napoleon greeted Owen with a slight bow of the head.

"Mr. Secretary," Owen replied.

Napoleon stared at Owen with an unnerving directness. It was like being appraised by an angel of dubious moral character. "I remember the day you left for Tiderealm with Ambassador Chetworth. When was it? Ninety-one? President Burgod remarked on your leaving, which must be why I recall it so clearly. *The boy is smarter than the ambassador,* he said to me. In my mind's eye I can still see you sitting dutifully in the carriage by Chetworth's side. I had paid scant attention to you until that moment. But I have paid attention ever since."

Owen measured his words before responding. "You pay me a great compliment. I wish that I could return the favor, but most of what I know of you I know from my father, and the stories he has shared are not in a similar vein."

Napoleon deflected the blow with the soft smile of a man accustomed to absorbing verbal arrows. "Your father and I did not see eye to eye often," he admitted. "I wish we had. We were both Baronites, were we not? It is best when Baronites stick together."

Owen nearly said, *The Baronite party is dead*, but instead opted for the more telling truth. "My father did not consider you a true Baronite."

That soft smile again, coupled with a bit lip. After a considerable pause, Napoleon changed the subject completely.

"The town is abuzz with news of your impending duels. Along with discussion of Senator Stevens's stroke, I've heard talk of little else."

"Yes. It's quite the spectacle."

"You'll be dueling with Wescos, I imagine?"

He means the pistol, Owen deduced at last. Dueling parlance was not Owen's lingua franca. "I don't know, truth be told. Isaiah Braswell is my second. We...we haven't spoken since the day the duels were arranged."

Napoleon gave Owen a look of genuine concern. "It will be Wescos. It always is. They're temperamental beasts. Be sure that you aim a little lower than your intended target, as most misses are high. Also, have Mr. Braswell check that your opponent's barrel hasn't been rifled beforehand. It's unlikely that they'd tamper with the guns, but I wouldn't rule it out entirely. When the duel begins, stand sideways, so as to provide a smaller target. If you both miss the first shot, loudly claim that your honor has been satisfied. That should put an end to it. If Mr. Luck insists on going forward with another round, and you are struck, the public will consider him a murderer. Which is why he'll claim that his honor has been satisfied as well, as long as you do it first."

Owen was taken aback, both by the depth of the knowledge Napoleon had provided him and by the realization that he was completely unprepared for the duel. He felt a wave of unexpected gratitude wash over him.

"Thank you," he said.

Napoleon gave a slight nod before placing an avuncular hand on Owen's arm. "As I said before, we Baronites must stick together." The expression on his face was heartfelt. "Stay alive next week, if at all possible."

Owen searched for the right words to best express his appreciation, but he couldn't think of them fast enough. Napoleon Wright released his arm and returned to the dark knot of conspirators at his table.

The din inside of Seford's suddenly spiked as dozens stopped listening in on their conversation and resumed their meals. Owen sighed.

So much for not being seen, he thought.

Nighttime arrived, and with it, no sign of Emmaline.

Owen lay in bed, a simple straw-stuffed cot in the far corner of the main room, his mind teeming with thoughts. They bounded around the inside of his skull like fleas on a mangy dog, disordered and uncontrollable.

Where is Emmaline? Is she in danger?

What will father say when he reads the letter? What will mother say? My sister?

What will it feel like if I am struck by a bullet?

Napoleon Wright has dueled before, hasn't he? Perhaps I should seek him out, ask for more advice of the kind he proffered today. I need to see him and Braswell both. But where is Isaiah? He's nearly as young and green as I am, a perfectly stupid choice for a second.

Damn! I forgot to visit the senator. Oh, what an ass I am. Here I am, his chief adjutant, and I wasn't there for him when he had the stroke, and I didn't stop by to console the family the day after. Father would be ashamed.

Father. If only he were here to advise me, but what advice could he even offer that would be of benefit? He never fought in a duel. In his day, Olgardians were too busy fighting the Sovereignty War to fight one another. Still, I would like to speak with him, if only to say goodbye.

Until then, another wordless conversation with the Stoneman's daughter would suit me. What a strange and wonderful creature she is. But where is she? Perhaps she left, perhaps I disappointed her in some way, perhaps she realized that staying here was a terrible error in judgement...

His thoughts were interrupted by the front door opening. Owen pushed up on his elbows, watching as the shadow of a young woman stepped in front of a great swath of exposed night sky. At first Emmaline moved like a thief, coming in quick and quiet, but, once inside, her movements became deliberate. She closed the door with a gentle and unhurried push, and then she turned and looked in Owen's direction, adjusting to the darkness of the room.

Together they navigated the distance, finding one another. Seconds became minutes, the time passing until there could be no doubt that she saw him as clearly as he saw her. Under cover of darkness, an intimacy grew between them, the type of bond that can only be formed in shadows and silence.

His heart thundered in his chest. He was certain that at any moment she would come to him.

But she didn't. Apropos of nothing, she looked away. Then, swift and quiet as a hare darting through the underbrush, she disappeared upstairs.

7

The remaining four days before Owen's duel with Jeremiah Luck rushed by in an anxious, lovesick blur.

The morning walk became a routine. Precious few words were exchanged between Owen and Emmaline during these outings, but the ones they did barter were of significant value. At the end of each walk, they held hands. Owen would feel it then: the magnetic attraction of their souls. But at the very moment that their intentions were aligned, something would shift, and Emmaline would move away from him. Twice, in the instant before Owen leaned in to kiss Emmaline, she dropped his hand and turned her head; and once, when he was about to put into words the maelstrom of emotions she had fomented in him, she cut him off with a proclamation of her own, a strange non sequitur about trees, of all things.

Come midday, they would go their separate ways.

Owen kept busy, primarily by meeting with Isaiah Braswell. Just as Napoleon Wright had predicted, Isaiah confirmed that the duel was to be fought with Wescos. To Owen's shock, Isaiah procured the set for practice (upon familiarizing himself with the code of the duel, Isaiah had discovered that both sides were to have equal access to the weapons beforehand). Together they fired the pistols into a copse of trees at the edge of the Potter estate.

Owen aimed low, as Napoleon Wright had advised. He hit his target two out of five times the first practice, three out of five times the second.

After the practice sessions, Isaiah informed Owen of the goings-on in the halls of government. It was a simple story, repeated: Briggs Shroud and the Free Harrish party continued to exercise absolute power. The only interesting tidbit was the news that Rufus Arry, and, to a lesser extent, Tyus Redgrave, appeared to be on the outs with party leadership. Isaiah claimed there was a rumor that President Randolph wanted Arry dismissed as vice president. Redgrave, while not on the verge of being kicked out of the party, had been reduced to spending his days sulking at his desk. "Shroud has stuck him in the corner for his misbehavior," Isaiah said. "But unlike with Arry, I do not believe that Tyus's detention is permanent."

On the second day of his interim, Owen visited Senator Stevens. The old battle horse was a paralytic husk of his former self. "The senator has only one battle left," Seth Templeton said to Owen in a hushed aside outside of the senator's room, while the senator's wife and daughter attended to Jude Stevens's delicate needs. Owen nodded sympathetically, not knowing what else to do. Before leaving, Owen promised that he would help out the family in any way possible, to which Seth nodded at Owen like he was a ghost. Owen left uncertain whether Seth considered his offering an empty gesture, or whether Seth simply thought Owen a walking dead man.

Otherwise, Owen's attentions centered on the Titan's Daughter. He found falling in love to be a fantastic distraction to the looming duel. Most days, Emmaline disappeared from midday until after dark, at which point she would return and the two of them would re-enact their intimate nighttime staredown. There was always a moment when Owen was certain that she would come to him, but the spell would always break. He was desperate to hold her, to touch her, to physically confirm what he knew was between them, but after the first couple of days, he understood that the decision was hers, and not his, to make.

The day before the duel, the routine broke.

Owen returned to the Potter guest house in the late afternoon following an in-town meeting with Isaiah Braswell. To his surprise and delight, he saw Emmaline through the front window as he walked up the dirt drive. Owen quickened his pace, thrilled by the prospect of spending the evening with her. He could think of no better way to spend what might be his final hours on the planet.

But when he opened the door, Emmaline was not alone. Standing beside her was Mathias Potter. Together, the two of them were studying a small object in Emmaline's hand. Owen, confused, stood in mute silence until his presence was registered. When they turned to face him, Mathias wore an inscrutable expression, while Emmaline secreted the object into a pocket on the inside of her buckskin dress.

The old man spoke first. "Good evening, Owen." He looked unspeakably happy and terribly tired all at the same time.

"Mr. Potter. I...I didn't expect to find you here."

Mathias Potter nodded. "Yes. I imagine not. But it is my house, all the same." The Baronite patriarch turned to Emmaline. He gave a small little sigh. "Thank you," he said. Then, without another word, he took his leave, moving past Owen with a turtle-like steadiness, out of the guest house and up the hill to his own abode.

Owen waited until the old fellow was out of earshot before speaking. "What did you show him?"

Emmaline didn't respond. But she met his eyes in a way that made it clear that she felt neither the need to explain, or to apologize.

The silent seconds wore at Owen. He had thought that the distance keeping them apart was gossamer-thin, that at any moment it might be bridged. But, having seen what he'd just seen, he understood it was greater than he had believed.

He spoke again, his voice near trembling. "I don't understand. Don't you know that you can trust me? Don't you know that—"

She finished his sentence for him. "That you love me?"

"I do love you."

A tear came to her eye. It bulged and then cascaded to the island of her cheek, sitting there like a pristine lake. "I'm leaving tonight. We may never see each other again."

He laughed a painful laugh. "I may die tomorrow. There was a good chance we'd never see each other again regardless."

She dipped her head a little as if to acknowledge that this was true. *Blunt truths,* he thought. *If only I could marry her, she would make a fine member of the Walsh family.*

She looked at him with sorrowful eyes. "If we do see each other again after tonight, and you decide that you still love me, then I swear to you that I will return your love with all of my heart."

"It's already done. I will love you always."

She didn't respond. Instead, she studied him silently. He studied her in turn. The brilliant sickle curve of her face. The way her wild brown hair lassoed around her neck.

Her eyes like fractured brown-green gemstones. The way she gazed at the world like a resting bird of prey.

Most of all he studied the wonder of her silence, how she held it in reserve like a fountain of power.

Suddenly she walked toward him. She didn't stop until they were face to face, their breath wrestling in the air between them. She studied him again at this closer distance for what felt like an eternity, and then she leaned forward and kissed him.

He slipped into the kiss's infinite promise. She did too, long enough for the truth of the kiss to hold its form.

Then she pulled away.

Looked away.

Walked away.

Out of the house and gone.

Nighttime arrived.

Owen sat up in bed, waiting. He knew the prospect of Emmaline's return was slim, but still he held vigil.

Outside, an armada of tufted clouds gave strength to a mighty darkness. Owen could sense a powerful energy gathering. *It's death,* he thought, *waiting for me.* To his surprise, he found he didn't care. He would gladly die tomorrow. If only he could see Emmaline again tonight.

Hours passed. His thoughts drifted into the strange borderland where memories danced with dreams. He saw Emmaline on the banks of the Marinus, attacking Lucien Gringer with the fearlessness of an ancient Ithiaian goddess. Next she was inside the Temple of the Bronze Titan, serving out her sentence for the crime of being brave. Without realizing it, Owen's thoughts tumbled into the slipstream. There he saw Charlsey Roges dying on the bed in Doc Bickerstaff's house, holding Chitniza's hand, while what appeared to be a panther prowled the room. Jude Stevens stood at the front of the Beacon, delivering a speech, but his mouth was sewn shut, and the sounds he made were muffled nonsense. Tyus Redgrave danced round a fire with Lucien Gringer and Jeremiah Luck, the three of them chanting Owen's name. And of course there was Emmaline, everywhere and nowhere at once, moving in and out of the corridors of Owen's mind, within his grasp and then gone again. His thought-dreams continued to tumble, tumble...until suddenly there was a moment of perfect clarity. Emmaline stood before him on the opposite bank of a wide and mighty river, radiant in sunlight. *She's waiting for me,* he understood. He moved into the waters, confident that he could cross...but when the water was up to his knees, he lost certainty...he looked back up to see that Emmaline was cast in shadow, a towering black in the form of a man...but it wasn't merely a man...the shadow swallowed Emmaline, growing evermore mythic and monstrous, branching out into...a pair of antlers.

He pulled out of the slipstream, gasping at reality with deep breaths. He tried to remember what he had seen, but already it was fading...

The last of the dream-vision disappeared as Owen came fully into the present. To his shock, he realized that he wasn't alone in the room. Emmaline was standing only a few feet from the bed, looking down at him.

Owen's breathing calmed. He found Emmaline's eyes in the darkness.

They spoke the concluding words of the silent conversation they'd been carrying on for days.

She took the final few steps to the bed. Slipped in beside him. She nestled her head on his chest while he encircled her body with his arm. He felt the rapid-fire beating of her hummingbird heart. Wherever she had come from, whatever she had done, she was still reliving its restive stirrings. He held her close with a perfect and gentle stillness. It was his last night on the planet, and he had all the time in the world.

Minutes passed. Maybe hours. A deep and restorative peace descended. Owen said a silent prayer to a nameless god.

Thank you.

He closed his eyes, content. But in that instant Emmaline lifted her head off his chest. Owen opened his eyes, and he and Emmaline found each other once more in the dark, this time from a distance not nearly so great.

Together they bridged the gap.

8

Owen started getting ready a little before sunrise. He dressed, ate a little bread and hard cheese, then set out on the road.

Isaiah Braswell was waiting for him at a prearranged spot on the western shores of the Marinus River. Together they navigated a rowboat across the breadth of the mighty waters, letting the current carry them south.

The sluggish day suddenly burst into being. The sun, obscured at daybreak by clouds, at last climbed the steps to its throne seat. With its scepter of rays, the sun pointed out all manner of beauty, from herons in flight to river otters on the hunt to the dazzling striations of rock that flowed from the foundation of the Beacon. Owen took one long last look at the seat of the Olgardian government as they rowed past, all manner of memory running through his mind. His gaze lingered on the grand platform at the back of the Beacon where his father had taken the oath of office six years earlier. In his mind's eye, Owen could still see Jude Stevens and Norman Burgod looking on while William Walsh swore to protect and defend the country.

All dead, or defeated, he thought.

He cut off the next thought before it swallowed him whole.

Shortly past the Beacon, around a bend in the river, Wandering Bluff swung into view on the eastern bank. The bluff was partially obscured by a wild tangle of trees jutting out of the hillside. The outcropping of rock that constituted the bluff proper looked more like a variance in the landscape than a distinct feature, which was the reason for the bluff's name. But, unfortunately, the bluff was as stationary as ever, and had not, as Owen had hoped, discovered a way to live up to its namesake.

They rowed a little past the bluff, and docked the rowboat on a dirt-rock shore. No other boat was in sight.

"We're first to arrive," Isaiah announced.

The two men followed a well-worn trail through the riverside woods to the top of the bluff. The view from on high was majestic and serene. *Not a bad place to die,* Owen thought, although now that he was here, the entire enterprise seemed the height of folly. *What creatures are we, to plot against each other in the midst of such beauty?* he wondered. Despite his efforts to guard against it, his thoughts brushed up against Emmaline.

What creatures are we, to kill each other in the midst of such love?

His musings were interrupted by the sight of a rowboat rounding the river bend. From his vantage point, Owen could see the men who intended to end his life.

Isaiah, standing nearby, spoke to Owen in a somber voice. "You are a good man, Owen Walsh. A good Baronite. But that doesn't mean you have to go willingly to the grave. Fire first, and fire straight. Put Luck down, and Redgrave and Gringer will go running."

Owen didn't respond. For days now he had mulled the options over in his head. The thought of killing a man sickened him, but the thought of standing there and simply hoping that he himself wasn't killed seemed even more disagreeable.

Down on the beach, three men exited the boat. Luck, Redgrave, and the Free Harrish physick who had attended to Senator Stevens when the senator had his stroke. Owen watched as the lordly lion tied the boat to a sapling on the shore. Looking closer, he noticed that something was amiss. Both Tyus and Jeremiah were struggling to stand fully upright; they leaned over at the waist as if sick at their stomach. When they began their trek up the hill, their struggles became even more apparent. Only the doctor looked healthy.

They were a sorry lot that reached the top. Luck's face was a wan yellow-green. It was difficult to make a similar assessment of Tyus's visage, as he had stopped shortly before the crest and was vomiting behind an evergreen.

"This is…unexpected," Isaiah said, as confused as Owen. "Perhaps we should offer to delay the duel until Jeremiah is recovered? It would be the honorable course."

"Yes," Owen replied, keeping his eyes fixed on his two adversaries.

Isaiah ventured forward. The physick moved to greet him. They had exchanged only a handful of words when Tyus Redgrave emerged from the woods holding the case with the dueling pistols, his face aflame with both fever and anger. He summoned a great deal of energy, and, pointing a finger at Owen, spewed a strange accusation.

"You aided that she-devil, you damnable bastard! You swore that you'd give her shelter. I heard it from Doc Bickerstaff's own lips. Now Lucien is dead, and you're harboring the Torquecan slut who poisoned us. But no amount of poison will spare your life today. Do you hear me, Walsh?"

Owen was beyond confused. "Lucien Gringer is dead?" he asked.

"He died last night," the physick explained. "Some Torquecan evil afoot, if reports are to be believed."

"Don't pretend that you weren't aware, you sun-devil lover!" Tyus bellowed. Vomiting appeared to have returned him some of his strength. "Rest assured that once you're dead, I'll find her! Then I'll kill her, but not before she's reminded what it is to be a slave!"

Chitniza, Owen understood. It was true, he had offered to help Chitniza and Charlsey escape from bondage, but that was before Charlsey had died and Chitniza spurned his offer. Now it seemed that Chitniza had killed Lucien Gringer, poisoned Tyus and Jeremiah, and gone into hiding. But how?

Owen turned to Jeremiah Luck, who was sitting on the ground with his head between his knees. *Better to address him than Tyus,* he thought. "Jeremiah, if you are ill, I am willing to postpone our duel to a later date. Or dismiss the duel altogether. Only say the word."

Jeremiah neither looked up nor responded.

Tyus, recovered enough to be enraged, half-barreled, half-lurched toward his friend. He opened the case with the dueling pistols, and, after hauling Jeremiah to his feet, began loading the firearms.

Isaiah sprang into action. "This is irregular!" Owen's friend shouted, marching toward Tyus. "The pistols are not to be loaded unless both seconds are supervising! I insist that you follow the code of the duel!"

The physick, flustered, turned his back on the proceedings.

Owen's heart beat ever harder and faster.

Jeremiah, listless, struggled to stand.

Tyus and Isaiah exchanged harsh words, then exchanged weapons. Isaiah eyeballed the barrels, checking that they were smoothbore.

Tyus leaned over at the waist and dry-heaved. He rallied to continue his duties.

Isaiah leaned in and spoke to Jeremiah, only for Tyus to put a heavy paw on his shoulder and push him away.

And with that, the huddle broke. Isaiah walked toward Owen, carrying one of the Wescos.

Isaiah looked troubled as he pressed the already-cocked pistol into Owen's hand. "We should have drawn lots for position. But Tyus has no patience for protocol. His only concern is your death." Owen's second gave him an earnest look. "You would be completely justified if you left the grounds. I would defend you in the court of public opinion."

Owen shook his head. "No. So long as Jeremiah stands with a gun in his hand, I will too."

Behind them, Tyus counted off paces. The already-positioned Jeremiah stood on his spot, waiting. Jeremiah looked like a pale ghost; even his rich, brown moustache had faded in the pallor of his illness.

"Here," Tyus grunted, motioning Owen to his spot. When Owen didn't move quickly enough for Tyus's liking, the young senator summoned a reserve of energy, and screamed, "Here!"

"You disgrace yourself, Senator Redgrave!" Isaiah admonished. But it was like arguing with a belligerent drunk. Tyus sneered, snorted, and swayed as Owen approached, only to give ground at the last moment and move to the middle distance between the two participants.

Owen stared down the line at his combatant. Jeremiah Luck, vaunted marksman, seemed barely capable of lifting his gun.

Have I been wrong about the outcome? Owen wondered. *Might I survive?*

Isaiah and Tyus moved perhaps some fifteen yards off the firing line. There they argued over a bit of dueling etiquette, an argument that, to Owen's surprise, Isaiah appeared to win.

Isaiah's voice carried over the gentle morning breeze. "Gentlemen, if you are ready, I will announce *Present*, and then the duel may commence. Are you ready?"

The moment is here, Owen realized. He turned sideways to present a smaller target.

"Ready," Jeremiah croaked. He continued facing Owen head-on.

When Owen responded, he felt as if he was using another man's voice. "Ready," he announced.

A smattering of birdsong colored the silence.

"Present!"

Owen fought the panicky urge to raise his pistol and fire. Instead, he watched his opponent's gun hand with hawk's eyes.

Jeremiah, drifting in his illness, kept the pistol by his side.

"Fire, damn you!" Tyus demanded of his friend.

Jeremiah's gun hand moved. But slowly, like the minute hand of a speeding wall clock, and away from Owen, toward the empty expanse to his right. Owen strained to hold his gun down, his muscles aching with the anticipation of being fired upon and needing to fire back. But hold it down he did, his eyes the tether to his impulses, refusing to accede to fears that his vision swore had not been made manifest.

Jeremiah's arm reached ninety degrees. The pistol rang out a loud but harmless note.

A lightheaded giddiness nearly overwhelmed Owen. He found his voice, said what needed to be said.

"My honor is satisfied," he shouted across the field. "Has your honor been satisfied, sir?"

"Yes," Jeremiah replied.

The first duel was over. And if Lucien Gringer truly was dead, Owen needed only survive one more.

Isaiah approached, a broad smile on his face. Over Isaiah's shoulder, the lordly lion snatched the dueling pistol from Jeremiah Luck's hand, but it was no concern of Owen's. Owen looked down at the pistol in his hand, still cocked. *Ha! I didn't even fire it.* He had the distinct feeling that the result would be different when he dueled against Tyus, but that was a week or more in the future, an eternity of time.

Isaiah grabbed Owen about the shoulders and shook him in a sort of giddy hug. The sober expression he had worn all morning was gone, replaced by a beaming countenance that called to mind the pageboy Isaiah had once been.

"You're alive!"

"Yes. Yes, it seems so."

Isaiah continued, verbalizing thoughts he'd until now had the grace to keep quiet. "No doubt your father will intervene before the next duel. I would imagine he's written to half of Centichester by now. I would not be surprised in the slightest if he arrives in town by the end of the week. There's a chance, once he's had his say…"

Isaiah didn't finish, but Owen knew what he was implying. William Walsh was a former president of the republic. He had friends, even among the hated Free Harrish. There was a possibility that William Walsh might convince one of them to intervene on Owen's behalf. A chance that he might convince one of them to persuade Tyus to withdraw his challenge.

It was possible that Owen's nightmare was over.

Owen glanced once more over Isaiah's shoulder. Jeremiah had retreated from the field and was stumbling down the bluff. Tyus had his back turned to Owen and was kneeling on the ground in front of the dueling pistols' case. Owen supposed he was grappling with another wave of sickness. The physick came into view, approaching Tyus from the young senator's right. Owen noticed that the doctor was staring at Tyus with a rather perplexed expression on his face.

"Senator Redgrave?" the physick asked. "Senator? What are you—why are you reloading—?"

Tyus struggled to upright. Turned.

Jeremiah's dueling pistol was in Tyus's hand. The trigger was cocked. Tyus waved it in the direction of Owen with all the menace his sick form could muster.

"This ends today, Walsh. We duel now."

Owen struggled to register what was happening.

Brave Isaiah jumped into action.

"Put down the gun, Redgrave!" Owen's second shouted, rushing toward Tyus. "This is unbecoming of—"

With an unnerving calmness and sudden physical possession, Tyus stepped toward the oncoming Isaiah Braswell and pressed the barrel of the pistol to his forehead. Isaiah smartly shut up, put his hands up, and backed away.

Owen recovered from being dumbstruck. He raised the still-cocked pistol in his hand and yelled at Tyus. "Face me, Redgrave! I'm the one you want!"

And so the young senator did. Tyus readjusted his posture and faced Owen, turning sideways into a dueling stance. "You're like your father, Walsh. You chose the wrong side of history. Now you will pay the price. Present!"

With a shock, Owen realized that Tyus had announced the start of his own duel. From a range of about twelve paces, Tyus raised his pistol. Owen, his dueling pistol already pointed at Tyus, caught a lightning bolt of memory—*aim a little low*—and he paid heed, slowing his breathing and lowering the gun, focusing on keeping his aim steady...and then he pulled the trigger. There was a flash—or was it two flashes?—followed by the bite of a thousand bee stings in Owen's right forearm.

Disoriented, Owen grimaced at the pain. There was a nasty wound perhaps six inches above his elbow. His forearm was on fire, but it appeared that only his arm was hurt, and nothing more.

Remembering Tyus, Owen looked through the diaphanous glaze of smoke. He saw no one. He wondered where Tyus had gone. A split second later, his vision adjusted, slightly to the left, and there he saw a man bleeding on the ground, a hand stanched to his stomach.

Owen dropped the Wesco. Isaiah approached, concerned, but even as he checked the damage to Owen's forearm, the two of them shambled toward Tyus Redgrave, knowing that his was the graver injury.

The physick was already kneeling beside the dying man, fingers feeling for a pulse. Owen stared, struggling to reconcile the vision of the mortally wounded man with his own decision to pull the trigger. Only seconds ago Tyus Redgrave had been his truculent, vainglorious self. Now he was a broken toy soldier: ponytail of dirty-blond hair splayed on the ground like chaff from the stalk, mangled at the core, lifeblood leaking onto the Olgardian soil.

As Owen stared, Tyus's consciousness waded to the surface of his dying waters. His eyes found Owen's.

"I didn't think you were capable," he said plainly.

Then he closed his eyes once more, and breathed his last.

9

"You work for the Free Harrish now?" Owen asked Gringold as they made their way through the pre-dawn streets.

"We all work for the Free Harrish now, Mr. Walsh," Gringold responded. "Like it or not."

They arrived at the Gray House before the sun was up, as requested by President Randolph. It felt good to be outside again. Owen had spent the two days since the duel holed up in the Potter guest house, tending to the gash in his arm and waiting for snippets of news from the outside world. Isaiah had stopped by twice, providing what insight he could to the public's reaction to Tyus Redgrave's death, and filling Owen in on the rumors circulating about Lucien Gringer's demise. At the end of the second visit, Isaiah informed Owen that President Randolph wanted to see him at the presidential mansion the following day. "He'll be sending an escort," Isaiah told him.

And so he had.

Gringold gave an embarrassingly heavy knock on the front doors. From the outside, the house looked largely the same as it had when Owen had lived there, though there were a few small changes. Owen had always thought it an ill-fitting abode for a president: unlike the Beacon, with its obvious Ithiaian—and therefore, republican—influences, the Grey House looked like the decadent but somewhat neglected estate of a landed lord from the old country (at least based on the books Owen had read). The grey stone gave it a gloomy feel, and there were numerous eccentric finishes unbecoming of a republican president, including the miniature pair of gargoyles staring down at Owen from the corners of the oak door frame. Owen's mother had done her best to minimize the effect of the house's peculiarities when the Walshes lived there, but now that Randolph was the resident, the structure seemed more in tune with its oddities, which made the house, on the whole, a more unsettling place than it had previously been.

To Owen's surprise, James Randolph himself opened the doors. Early as it was, the president was entirely put together. His infamous red hair was plaited to perfection, he was clothed in a smart but unassuming fashion, and his expression, though consciously empty, could not conceal the deep and burning intelligence behind his eyes.

"Good morning, Mr. Walsh," the president said, giving a slight bow of his head.

"Good morning, Mr. President."

President Randolph turned to Gringold. "Thank you, sir. It seems your reputation as a man who can be relied upon is well earned. With your permission, I will call upon you again in the future."

"As you wish, Mr. President," Gringold responded with a surprising formality. Hearing Gringold strike the subservient tone lanced Owen's heart. *What Gringold said is true,* Owen thought. *We all work for the Free Harrish now. Like it or not.*

Owen followed the president inside as Gringold departed. "We'll sit in the library," Randolph suggested as they wound their way toward the back of the mansion, down halls that, to Owen's pleasant surprise, were framed with many of the same paintings and documents that had graced the mansion during William Walsh's term. *Though of course he'll have removed father's copy of Baron Dyrirnotic's The Spiriting Principles,* Owen was certain, only to turn the corner and find the first page of Dyrirnotic's most famous work on the same wall space where his father had left it, at the corner of the hall leading to the library, at a vantage where it was nearly impossible to miss.

Owen stopped and stared at the framed page on the wall, too flabbergasted to move on. President Randolph stopped with him.

"Is this father's?" Owen asked.

James Randolph brought a finger to his chin and smiled. "Yes. He left it here. When I saw it, I thought it well placed." He tapped the finger on his chin once, then twice. Then he began a most unexpected story. "Your father and I spent time in Trufic together, in the years before the Sundering. Were you aware?"

Owen nodded uncertainly. His father talked often enough of his time as a diplomat in the old world, and it was common knowledge that James had been there at the same time. What Owen didn't know was the scope of their partnership. "I've heard bits and pieces."

"When the Sovereignty War ended, there was an extended idyll where the two of us had little pressing work. Together we took a trip to the south, and visited Baron Dyrirnotic's home. Dyrirnotic had died years before, but his widow was still alive. When she learned who we were, she plied us with wine, olives, and cheese. Then she handed over Dyrirnotic's original manuscript of *The Spiriting Principles,* with his notes in the margins. We drank little of the wine, mind you. Neither your father nor I wanted our senses dulled while we perused a genius's work. We spent the remainder of the afternoon in a state of pure intellectual bliss. For days after we conversed about nothing save how best to apply what we had learned into the building of our new nation. To this day, it's one of my fondest memories."

Owen stared at the president, dumbstruck. "You called Baron Dyrirnotic a genius. If you were to say that in the company of those in your party—"

"—I would not say it, of course," the president interrupted. "Not in public, at least." The president motioned toward the library. "Let's take a seat before we continue. Discussing political matters while standing has always felt a bit barbaric to me."

They entered through large oak doors with glass-inlay paneling. The library, to Owen's wonderment, was packed with even more books than it had been during his father's tenure. Two of the bookshelves had been extended, and there was a new addition, a curving piece cut from an unfamiliar wood that was wedged into the far corner of the room. It held an impressive number of books.

"That particular bookshelf is made from jorkwood, a tree found in Wolfresh," the president said when he saw Owen looking at it. "Please, take a seat."

Owen did as he was told. The president arranged himself on the opposite side of the large mahogany desk. Behind President Randolph, through a large wood-paneled window, Owen could see the Grey House gardens, a lovely blend of Olgardian trees and flowers manicured to perfection. It reminded Owen of why the library had been his father's favorite room when he was president. It was one of the only places where William Walsh could find a respite from his responsibilities.

"I trust your arm is healing," President Randolph said. "I heard that you suffered a wound."

Owen instinctively brought his left hand to the place where his right arm had been gashed by the lead musket ball from Tyus Redgrave's pistol. The providence that prevented the ball from doing more damage seemed, in retrospect, divine in nature.

"Yes. A small flesh wound. I was fortunate."

James Randolph considered this. In his meditative state, the president looked, as he often did, somewhat inhuman, a creature too attuned to the metaphysical to be made of flesh and bone.

"The country was fortunate. You are an intelligent and talented young man. Our young nation can ill-afford to lose its brightest minds."

Owen didn't know how to respond. The comment was entirely unexpected, especially considering that Tyus Redgrave was dead.

"Would that no one had died," the president continued, seemingly covering for his omission. "Although, based on what I've heard, no one bears as much responsibility for Tyus Redgrave's death as Tyus Redgrave. Lucien Gringer's passing, on the other hand, is an entirely different matter. The dark reports that I've heard are troubling, to say the least."

"Yes, Mr. President," Owen replied, keeping his response vague. He had heard the rumors as well, from Isaiah. It seemed the city was abuzz with talk of Torquecan magic: numerous people had sighted a panther prowling the streets of Centichester the night that Lucien passed, and word was that Lucien had been mauled to death during his sleep. The general consensus was that the panther was a Torquecan god come to life; most believed it had been summoned by the contracted Torquecan woman who disappeared the same night. Chitniza. Owen's promise to help Chitniza escape Tiderealm was no doubt making the rounds in certain Free Harrish circles, but, in truth, Owen was as ignorant of her location as the next man.

The president fixed Owen with a long, searching stare. Owen had no doubt that the president had heard the rumors as well. At last, James Randolph seemed to reach some conclusion. "For multiple reasons—Tyus Redgrave's death not least among them—there are those in my party who, were they to encounter you in public, would feel obliged to challenge you to a duel. I believe these are fleeting passions. There are very few who held true affection for the young senator. Given enough time, there will come a day when you will once more be able to walk the streets of Centichester without fear of losing your life." He paused. "Given enough time, I mean to put end to this barbaric dueling business once and for all."

"My father would approve," Owen said.

James Randolph gave a small, flat smile. "Yes. He would." The president opened a drawer on his side of the desk and pulled a letter from inside. "Speaking of your father, I received this letter from him yesterday. In it, he requested that, out of respect for our past friendship, I take whatever measures are in my power to ensure that you do not lose your life in the coming weeks."

Owen was unsurprised. He had received his own letter from his father yesterday, a long-winded screed that bespoke nothing so much as William Walsh's frustration at his inability to influence events from afar. In it, the former president swore that he meant to travel to Centichester as fast as possible.

President Randolph continued. "I will be honest. Had events not transpired as they did, I would have been disinclined to intervene. The political price would have been too high. But now that Mr. Redgrave and Mr. Gringer are deceased, I find it in my purview to affect matters in a way that will not only keep you from harm, but also be of benefit to the country."

Owen furrowed his eyebrows. He felt a flash of anger. "Be of benefit to the country? As I am a Baronite, I can only assume that you mean you see an opportunity to remove me from politics altogether?"

"On the contrary. I intend to send you to Tiderealm as part of a diplomatic envoy to the court of King Hugo Whesker."

Owen was too stunned to respond.

The president continued. "I may have upheld the peace treaty your father struck with King Hugo, but my party's position on the matter during the most recent election did considerable damage to our relationship with Tiderealm. You were the personal secretary to a Tiderealm ambassador during the Burgod administration, and you are the son of President Walsh. As such, you have both experience in Tiderealm and a political background that isn't reflexively anathematic to King Hugo's court. Your country needs your talents now to preserve the peace. We have rising tensions to the south and to the west. We can ill-afford a war with our rivals to the east."

Owen grasped for an appropriate response.

"I wasn't expecting...who else will make up the envoy?"

The president, a man of excessive composure, suddenly seemed, if anything, even more composed.

"George Pickwin." *A retired Free Harrish Senator.* "Abel Francis." *The former governor of the province of Barrensly.* "And Napoleon Wright."

It was to be a day of grand surprises, then.

"Napoleon Wright? I...how is that even...the other members of your party..."

"Mr. Wright is traveling with the envoy as an advisory member only. And you will be traveling as the junior member to a distinguished pair of diplomats, both of whom won't hesitate to pull rank should the need arise. Rest assured, Mr. Walsh, neither you nor Mr. Wright will have the power to undermine any decision Mr. Pickwin and Mr. Francis make. That being said, Napoleon Wright has cultivated hundreds of contacts within the Tiderealm aristocracy that might prove useful, and, as I said earlier, your pedigree and experience should prove invaluable. Were the mission objective something other than preserving your father's peace, I would, for obvious reasons, choose someone else. But, as our interests our aligned, and I consider you to be an intelligent and patriotic young man, I'm asking you for your service."

Owen was too dumbstruck to respond. He was to serve on behalf of the Free Harrish government? Suddenly the ramifications of what he would be agreeing to hit home. He was a Baronite, for Titan's sake. The Free Harrish were the enemy, the Slavocracy; they had destroyed everything Olgard might have been under Baronite rule, and now Owen was to simply switch sides and do President Randolph's bidding? Perhaps Napoleon Wright could sell his soul, but Owen wasn't that self-servingly malleable. He would turn it down, he would—

"Before you reply, Owen, if I may."

118

Owen surfaced from his contemplations. Looking up, he saw that President Randolph's customary cool diffidence was absent. Instead, a surprisingly earnest expression adorned the president's face. It disarmed Owen completely.

"You hesitate because you are a Baronite," the president said. "It's understandable. Admirable, even. You are loyal, both to your father and to your party. But you must know that the Baronite party is dead. It may continue to exist in the north for some time, but make no mistake: it will never be a national party again."

Owen knew that the president was right. But that didn't mean Owen had to confirm it with his own tongue.

The president continued. "But you—you are a young man at the outset of your political life. A man possessive of gifts and a family name that will not permit you to sit idly by while the battle for the heart and soul of the country rages on. This is why you must not pass up this opportunity. Soon, the party politics of today will be forgotten, and all that will be remembered are those who helped shape the destiny of our nation. You cannot do that in Centichester at the present moment, but you can help shape Olgard's future by going to Tiderealm. So go. Step away from the Olgardian shore while the Free Harrish tide sweeps in, and return a more powerful man than when you left, untouched by the damage. Then, when you are back home, see where the sands have settled, and make your mark once more."

"But my father—"

"—Your father was no party man. Oh, he was a Baronite in principle through and through, but he always believed political parties were a danger to the country. I would even venture that he'll give you his blessing. And understand—I'm not asking you to switch parties. I'm only asking you to protect the peace with Tiderealm. You may serve as a representative of the Olgardian government, but you will also be free to obey the dictates of your conscience. As a Walsh, I would expect you to do no less."

Owen sat with the president's words, letting them sink in. Perhaps what President Randolph said was true. There was nothing for Owen in Centichester. Going to Tiderealm was one of the few ways that he could continue serving the country. And the president had spoken truly about Owen's father. How many times had William Walsh chafed against the restrictions of party politics? *They mean to hang Dyrirnotic around my neck like a yoke,* President Walsh had complained more than once when his policy proposals were bucked by party members with a rigid Baronite worldview. But now, with the Baronite party all but dead, Owen would be free to go to Tiderealm as his own man. And if he was truly free to follow his beliefs, then…

"I will do it," he said. "But I will speak my mind. Often if need be. I won't go out of my way to undermine Mr. Pickwin and Mr. Francis, but neither will I stand idly by if I find that they mean to weaken my father's peace by other means."

"Good," the president replied. "Then we are of one mind. A defense of your father's peace treaty is a defense of my administration's policies. I implore you to defend it with all gusto."

A passing quiet settled in the room. Across the desk, the president sat with his fingertips pressed together beneath his chin, looking an exemplar of the sensible, diplomatic statesman. Owen felt himself succumbing to the satisfaction of their seeming accord. But he also knew that this was the same president who had encouraged his party to rail against the Walsh peace treaty for the purposes of winning the presidency. Owen refused to let it pass unremarked upon.

"I'm glad that I can be of service to the country, Mr. President. But, both as a Baronite and as my father's son, I would be remiss if I did not express my displeasure at your willingness to undercut the treaty when it suited your political ends, only to about face and defend it once you obtained the presidency. It was vile politics, sir, and unbecoming of a man of your stature."

Owen knew as soon as he said it that perhaps it was a blow too hard. *So be it,* he thought, as he waited for President Randolph's response. The president suffered the assault with characteristic composure, his initial response being to not respond at all. Owen waited as the president held himself with a perfect stillness; the only movement Owen detected was an imagined grinding of the mighty machinery of gears in James Randolph's mind.

At last the president broke off his impassive stare and looked to the right, remembering. Then he began a story.

"One day in Trufic, toward the end of my time in the country, your father and I became engaged in a very animated discussion with the Marquis de Taranok about how the concept of power might evolve in our newly sovereign nation. I was of a mind that our new government, being founded on the ideals of Great Awareness thinkers such as Dyrirnotic and Key, would breed men styled in the republican fashion, men who, though ambitious, would resist the worst power-grabbing impulses of the old world. Your father, to my surprise, took the side of the marquis. 'No, James,' I remember him saying to me, 'all that we can do is create laws to restrain men and then enshrine those laws in our constitution. But don't delude yourself into believing that the men themselves will be any different. We must see to it in our republic that we set an equitable playing field that encourages men of merit to take the field. Whatever happens after, is fair game.'

"Your father was right, of course," the president continued, turning and looking at Owen. Owen was hypnotized by the president's eyes. Their color had changed. He couldn't remember what color they usually were, but now they were a deep and startling red. Immediately Owen thought of Briggs Shroud on the day of Senator Stevens's stroke. "We might set the rules differently in our republic, but the fight for power remains the same as it has throughout the annals of human history. It's a ruthless, winner-take-all contest. In my life, I've had to learn that lesson many times over, but now, at last, I believe I've learned it for good. You'll have to learn it yourself one day, I imagine. When that day comes, you may judge me differently."

The room pulsed with a strange energy. Owen, still hypnotized, was stunned by a flashbang moment when, all at once, three changes to President Randolph took place simultaneously: the president's eyes exploded in flame, the president's hair crackled with color, and what appeared to be blood pooled at the edges of the president's mouth. But before Owen could react to or even comprehend what he had seen, James Randolph's appearance reverted to its normal form, so quickly that Owen doubted his own senses. The occurrence seemed as implausible as a bolt of lightning on a clear and cloudless day.

Owen gaped at President Randolph, but he didn't speak. The president, ever measured, returned Owen's stare with cool aplomb. When a sufficient amount of time had passed, the president took up the conversation once more.

"Power, I've discovered, comes in many different forms," the president said. "But I've found one in particular to be more effective than the others."

Later, when Owen was returning home, he found that his memories of the conversation with the president were fuzzy and unclear. He was to go to Tiderealm to defend his father's peace treaty—that he understood—but there was something else the president had asked of him, some bit of business that was both vitally important and entirely inconsequential. "You'll remember it when the time comes," President Randolph had assured Owen when he had left, with a confidence that only increased Owen's unease.

Back at the Potter place, Owen sat on the edge of his bed and racked his brain, but nothing came to him. He remembered taking the president to task for using the Tiderealm peace treaty as a political cudgel, but, as to what occurred afterward, Owen couldn't say. All Owen knew was that he had the unsettling suspicion that he had been manipulated somehow. But the details eluded him: the memory would form at the edge of his consciousness, but when he gave it his attention, it was like trying to make sense of an ill-formed shape in fog.

After an hour or so, he gave up. He lay back on his bed and offered his thoughts to the void. Once surrendered, Owen's thoughts passed by him like clouds, some borne away on zephyrs, others plodding by as if in a slow-moving parade. Eventually Owen slipped into the world of reveries, and there he discovered a different memory than the one he was searching for.

It was the night before the duel. He was lying in bed with Emmaline. Outside, dawn approached. He knew that in a couple of hours he might be dead, but all that mattered to him were the precious few minutes he had remaining with the Titan's Daughter.

She was the first to move. He felt his heart tear in two as she slipped out of bed and back into her buckskin dress. "Don't," he managed to say, ineffectual as he knew it would be. She turned and found him in the pre-dawn dark, a ghost already, the silhouette of love lost. He couldn't see her face clearly, but he sensed the pain in it, a pain that somehow both alleviated and increased his own. He wanted more than anything to call her back to bed, to keep her there until the end of time. But time and circumstances had conspired against them from the outset. They may have won a battle the previous night, but there was no changing the tide of the war.

Only, to his surprise, Emmaline did come back to bed. But not to lie with him. Instead, she sat beside him and, strangely, withdrew a small object from a pocket on the inside of the dress. Holding the object, she made a small sound. It took Owen a moment to realize that she was crying.

He placed his hand on the small of her back. "What is it?" he asked. She looked at him but she didn't answer. Instead, she turned her attention back to the object—which Owen now realized was a stone—and began turning it over and over, ever faster. She started speaking, but not to reply. Instead she repeated one word: *Dachahelu*.

124

The Deer King appeared in the stone. There was no mistaking who it was. The figure in the stone was only a child, but the antler nubs on its crown were already prominent, two bulging mounds showing the first signs of bifurcation. The Deer King's expression was at once both serene and wild, and, even across whatever distance the stone had bridged, it was evident that the child's power was palpable, a mighty current of force awaiting the hour of its manifestation. Looking at the Deer King, Owen experienced a sensation of vertigo; he felt as if he was standing on the edge of mankind's precipitous future, with the sense that all might fall.

The stone moved, a gentle tugging. Requesting some unknown end.

Emmaline stopped turning the stone. The Deer King disappeared.

For a moment they sat together in silence. Owen knew that what Emmaline had shared could not be unshared. She had given part of her burden to him, and, for the rest of his life, whether it was a matter of hours or years, he would have to live with the knowledge of both the Deer King's existence and Emmaline's ability to locate the Massaporan god.

But he was glad that she had done it. They were tied together now, more than they had been before. And they were tied to the Deer King too. Though perhaps that had always been the case. Owen knew from what he had seen that the child was a great power, and great powers weren't easily avoided in this world. His father had once told him that the only thing a person could do in the presence of power was face it with a brave heart and a nimble mind. And if, at the end, the power overcame you, so be it. Only take what wisdom you can from it as you go, even if that's on your way to the next life.

Owen opened his eyes. The last moments of his time with Emmaline played out in his mind: no words, only the stone slipped back into the buckskin pocket and a kiss, and then she was gone, out the door and into the morning dark to face all the awesome powers of existence.

He sat up in bed.

He knew that he would have to do the same.

Author's Note

Hey everyone! Thanks so much for reading *Last of the Baronites*. If you'd like to help the series grow, I'd be forever appreciative if you'd take the time to review this book and the other books in the series over at Amazon and Goodreads. Thanks again!

The Deer King: Novella One

The Sundering: Novella Two

Cast of Characters

Primary Characters

Owen Walsh – Adjutant to Senator Stevens; son of William Walsh, 2nd president of the Olgardian republic.

Emmaline Rain – Titan's Daughter, The Stoneman's Daughter

Charlsey Roges – A man of mixed ethnicity

Chitniza – Torquecan woman, contracted worker to Amelia Redgrave

William Walsh – 2nd president of Olgard

James Randolph – 3rd president of Olgard

Jude Stevens – Baronite senator, Owen Walsh's superior

Tyus Redgrave – Free Harrish senator, son of the late Secretary of State Daniel Redgrave

Isaiah Braswell – Adjutant to Senator Thumb of the Baronite Party; Owen Walsh's friend

Mathias Potter – Baronite Party patriarch; identical twin to Brigand Potter, who killed Yestric, the 4th Deer King.

Napoleon Wright – Former Secretary of the Treasury under Norman Burgod

Gringold – A toughman who often works on behalf of the Baronite Party

Other Characters

Lucien Gringer – Harrish man engaged to Amelia Redgrave

Jeremiah Luck – Friend of Lucien Gringer and Tyus Redgrave

Rufus Arry – Vice President of Olgard

Duncan Broggs – Editor of the *Anti-Monarchist Herald*, second to Lucien Gringer

Doc Bickerstaff – Centichester physician in good standing with the Baronite Party

Cornelia Stevens – Jude Stevens's wife

Constance Stevens Templeton – Jude Stevens's daughter

Seth Templeton – Jude Stevens's son-in-law

Priest Debin – A young priest of the Bronze Titan

Snowy Sam Girt – A bartender at Seford's Place

Abner Cox – Adjutant to Briggs Shroud

Senator Briggs Shroud – Free Harrish senator, Senate majority leader

Senator Moxley – Baronite senator

Senator Thumb – Baronite senator

Senator Whitestone – Baronite senator

Senator Sterling Holmes – Free Harrish senator

Senator Edward Mountbain – Free Harrish senator

Senator Paul Thomas Tice – Free Harrish senator

Senator George Conway – Free Harrish senator

Characters Mentioned But Did Not Appear

Brigand Potter – Identical twin to Mathias Potter, founder of the Baronite Party in Olgard, killed Yestric, the 4th Deer King

Norman Burgod – 1st president of Olgard

Amelia Redgrave – Sister of Senator Tyus Redgrave

Baron Dyrirnotic – Famed Trufic Philosopher during the Great Awakening, author of *The Spiriting Principles*

Gerald Key – Famed Harrish Philosopher during the Great Awakening

High Priest Musk – High Priest of the Bronze Titan

Claius Caya – Ithiaian emperor of yore

Gabriella – Mathias Potter's niece and caretaker

Abigail Walsh – Owen Walsh's sister

Ambassador Chetworth – Ambassador to Tiderealm during the Burgod administration

George Pickwin – Former Free Harrish senator

Abel Francis – Former governor of the province of Barrensly

Marquis de Taranok – Nobleman from Trufic